LEVELING
the field

A GAMERS NOVEL

MEGAN ERICKSON

Entangled Publishing, LLC
2614 South Timberline Road
Suite 109
Fort Collins, CO 80525
Visit our website at www.entangledpublishing.com.

Brazen is an imprint of Entangled Publishing, LLC. For more information on our titles, visit www.brazenbooks.com.

Edited by Heather Howland
Cover design by Heather Howland
Cover art from Taria Reed/The Reed Files

Manufactured in the United States of America

First Edition May 2016

ENTANGLED
BRAZEN

Dear Reader,

Thank you so much for accepting a series full of nerdy characters who often lack decent social cues. This series was fun, and I'm so happy you all came on the ride with me. I hope Ethan's book is fitting, and that you fall in love with Lissa as much as I did.

Megan

To everyone who waited a year to see Ethan get his happily ever after…

Chapter One

The guy was late.

Lissa Kingsman glanced at the clock on the wall of the office and tried not to look as irritated as she felt.

It was hard, though, because this day was simply not her day. First, she'd woken up with a headache that pain meds had just barely taken the edge off of, then her favorite barista wasn't at Queenie's Coffee and the substitute had messed up a simple latte.

Now she was standing in the conference room of *Gamers* magazine with a real-life Ken doll and the most annoying journalist to ever journal.

The only reason she hadn't left yet was, A) that would be unprofessional, and B) her friend Chad had promised her the guy who'd yet to show his face would be a perfect candidate for her project.

She tugged on a strand of her black curls and cracked her gum. Loudly.

Steven, the journalist writing the article about *Gamers* for the local newspaper, widened his eyes. Whoops, that might have been a little obnoxious.

Ken Doll, or Grant Osprey as he'd introduced himself, looked at her with amusement and a little bit of solidarity. Lissa decided she liked him.

"He said he'll be here soon," he said with a bright white smile.

Lissa cracked her gum again and raised her eyebrows.

He barked out a laugh and turned to look out the windows of his office.

She sighed and peered at the LCD screen on the back of her camera, flipping through pictures she'd taken yesterday. She wasn't a journalist, but she freelanced often as a favor to her long-time friend Sal, who ran the art team at the *Willow Park Daily*.

Her passion was portrait photography, and her current project was everyday people who bore scars—whether from surgery or a car accident or something else—and listening to their stories. When she'd seen the *Gamers* shoot on the newspaper's art department schedule, she hadn't been interested in taking the job until she'd mentioned it to Chad, knowing his sister worked at the magazine. Chad had told her he thought Ethan Talley, part owner of *Gamers*, would be perfect for Lissa's project.

Which was why she needed to be Charming Lissa today. Not Gum-Smacking Attitude Lissa.

She spit her gum into a napkin and threw it into the nearby trash can.

Letting her camera hang from her neck, she crossed her arms over her chest and gazed out the window.

A large black SUV pulled into the parking lot. The door opened, and a man stepped out, dark sunglasses protecting his eyes from the fall sun. He wore a black suit. Black shirt. Black tie. Black on black on black. His hair was black. The only thing that *wasn't* black was his skin, which was actually quite pale.

As he closed the door to his vehicle and the car beeped as the locks engaged, Lissa straightened and took a step closer to the window. In the background, she heard Steven and Grant talking softly, but her gaze was on the man now walking toward the building.

He was tall, very tall, with broad shoulders, and his stride was smooth—all long-legged and confident.

Lissa's knees went a little weak and her heart beat faster in her chest. Who was this guy? She had a thing for a man's walk. It was weird, beyond weird, but she loved to watch men walk. A hesitant gait turned her off, but a masculine strut like this guy? It revved *all* her engines.

Her sister used to tell her she should just check a man's teeth as if he was a horse if she was that into a guy's walk. Lissa used to tell her to shut up. Of course, if she could talk to her sister one more time, she certainly wouldn't be saying "shut up."

At that memory, Lissa squeezed her eyes shut, her arousal effectively doused as a wave of grief passed over her like it always did when she thought of her sister.

She took a couple of calming breaths and then opened her eyes to see the man opening up the front door of *Gamers*. It would be just her luck if he was the less-than-punctual Ethan Talley. She turned from the window and clutched her camera, the grip familiar and comforting, as loud footsteps came closer to the conference room.

Grant's head went up at the sound and he smiled. "Ah, Ethan's here."

Lissa sucked in a breath as a shadow crossed the threshold, because yes, he certainly was.

He stood in the doorway of the conference room, his hands hanging loose at his sides, his feet braced apart in their polished black shoes. His sunglasses were in his right hand, his ice-blue eyes surveying the room in a sweep until they finally landed on…her.

Did she imagine the slight stiffening in his body at the sight of her?

She blinked, willing herself to maintain a passive expression while she took in the scars that crept up his neck and along his jaw like flames.

Oh yes, she very much wanted to photograph him and learn his story. Except this guy didn't look forthcoming at all. His jaw was tight, his hands clenched so hard she feared he'd break his sunglasses, and his eyes were shards of ice. His gaze darted to Grant. "What's she doing here?"

Lissa jolted, every instinct screaming at her to tell this prick to go to hell, talking about her like she wasn't in the room. He was either a misogynist, a dick, or a racist at the sight of her black skin. Why hadn't Chad warned her?

Grant held up a hand. "Now, Ethan. This is good publicity for us. They want to take our picture for—"

"No picture," Ethan growled. There was really no other way to describe it. He growled.

Lissa was no stranger to people who were opposed to having their picture taken. It happened a lot when she took photos for the newspaper, but she hadn't expected this here. At all. Grant had reached out to the newspaper for an article, so she'd assumed everyone would be okay with her presence.

Not so much.

She needed to take control of the situation, so she stepped forward with her hand out. "Hi, I'm Lissa Kingsman."

He stared at her hand like it would poison him. Finally he reached out and clasped it, shaking it firmly, never taking his eyes off her camera, as if at any minute, it would begin to snap away. He said with hesitation, "Ethan Talley."

There was something familiar about his voice, and Lissa wracked her brain trying to place it.

He dropped her hand and moved to sit down beside Grant. "I'm not comfortable with this."

"Ethan," Grant said, clapping him on the shoulder. "Let's just talk to the reporter first and then we'll deal with the picture thing, okay?"

Ethan nodded with a jerk of his chin.

Lissa stepped back, wishing she could blend into the walls behind her, because Ethan was still watching her, like she was going to steal something from him. Like his picture.

O-kay. Forget considering him for her project—this was like dealing with a startled deer. She shoved her hands into her pockets so they weren't anywhere near the shutter button. He relaxed a fraction but still kept her in his line of sight.

Apparently, Steven had done some of the interview over the phone and was now asking some follow-up questions.

Lissa concentrated on Ethan's deep voice, which lost some tension as he talked about *Gamers* and something about finding a personality to be the face of the company on social media sites like YouTube.

Wait a second…

Just like that, Ethan's identity hit her like a brick to the chest. He was E-Rad, the video game commentator her younger brother had listened to non-stop as a teenager. E-Rad had made millions recording himself playing video games and putting the videos up on YouTube. His good looks and charming personality won him a huge following—both male and female—and even Lissa had a crush on him all those years ago. She hadn't recognized him when he'd walked in, maybe because of his scars or because he was a decade older than he'd been when he stopped making videos and disappeared from the gaming community.

It took all her strength and willpower not to point at him and yell, "Oh my God, you're E-Rad!" The guy hated her already because of the camera she wore around her neck.

And what if she was wrong?

But the more he talked, the more sure she was that he was E-Rad. If he would only let her take his picture… He probably had an amazing story to tell. Did those scars have anything to do with his vanishing act all those years ago?

Determination fired on all cylinders in her gut, and she swallowed. She *would* find a way to get this guy to agree. A high-profile person like him would garner attention for her project. And the more attention she got, the more money she would raise for the scholarship in honor of her sister.

So she straightened away from the wall and smiled her most charming Lissa Kingsman smile. Ethan's eyes narrowed on her, and she geared up for battle.

• • •

She was like Aphrodite with a hissing cobra wrapped around her neck.

Ethan wasn't sure what he wanted to do more—kiss her or throw her camera through a window.

His glare, his do-not-touch posture, had been honed for over a decade. It was incredibly effective to everyone but the gorgeous woman who stood in the room with her smooth dark skin, crimson lips, and short curly hair that framed a beautiful face.

It had been…too long to even mention since a woman had stirred his libido like this, and of course she had to want something from him. Something he hadn't been willing to give for a very long time.

Ethan shifted in his seat and scowled. It was bad enough he had to see his scars in the mirror every day. The last thing he wanted was photographic evidence of them, a tangible portrait of what he looked like to everyone else. Hell no. He also worried someone would recognize him from the days he made his fortune in front of a video camera. No one but his close friends and business partners knew about his past, and he preferred to keep it that way.

The reporter was wrapping up his questions, and Ethan smoothed down his black tie, ready to bolt, when a firm hand gripped his wrist. He turned to Grant, ready to snarl.

"We'll have her take some pictures of just me first, then us together, okay?" his friend asked.

Okay. That gave him more time to stall and come up with an excuse to leave, so he nodded and followed along as they all trouped to Grant's office.

Lissa stepped forward, her movements graceful, like a dancer's. Her red-painted toes peeked out from under a long purple skirt. As she fiddled with the knobs on top of her camera, a large collection of bangles clicked together on her forearm.

Large hoop earrings swayed as she held up the camera to her eye and directed Grant. The man smiled as he stood casually behind his desk, one hand braced on the back of his burgundy leather chair.

Despite the objects in the room—chairs, bookcases, a plant—Lissa moved around the room nearly silently, without bumping into anything.

Ethan couldn't take his eyes off her, especially when she bent over to get a different angled shot, which put her very round ass right in his line of vision.

He needed to take his jacket off, or loosen his tie, because his heart was pumping hot, hot blood faster and faster and it was all heading right down to…his cock.

Oh, so *now* his libido decided to wake up. Fuck it all.

He stood behind a chair in a corner, hoping it hid the evidence of his arousal. The reporter had left and, as it was a Sunday, the office was deserted. It was just Grant, Ethan, and this woman who was making him harder and harder with every glance out of her kohl-lined eyes.

And then she turned to him fully, the camera held out at her side. She licked her lips, a swipe of that pink tongue on her full red lips. "Are you ready?"

He was going to pass out, and then he'd wake up and kill Grant. His friend should have warned him about the picture thing. Hell, this was why he'd avoided just about any sort of gathering lately, including their friends' engagement party. He'd have to attend Marley and Austin's wedding in a couple of weeks, but he wasn't thinking about that right now.

He gripped the back of the chair in front of him until he felt the fabric begin to give away under his blunt nails. His heart pounded from anxiety, and his cock pressed against the zipper in his suit pants…and he was all about conflicting emotions today, apparently.

He was unsettled.

He didn't like feeling unsettled. And the source of that was in front of him right now, a hand on her hip, one perfect dark eyebrow raised at him.

With a finger pointed at Grant's chest, he said, "I told you no pictures. And I meant it." Then he turned to Lissa and tipped his head. "I'm sorry. Good luck with the article."

And then, before anyone could call him back, he strode from the room. He was almost to the front door when fast footfalls sounded behind him. He looked over his shoulder to see a camera-less Lissa jogging after him. "Hey!" she called.

He whirled around, twisting his face into the glare that had always served him well. Except around her apparently, because as she came to a halt in front of him, her skirt swirling around her legs, she didn't look scared at all. In fact, she looked pissed. "You know," she said, crossing her arms over her chest, which only succeeding in drawing his gaze to her cleavage. "It's kinda rude to bail on your business partner."

She pursed those pretty lips, and even with the horrible

fluorescent lights in the ceiling of the office, she was gorgeous. Her long lashes fanned out over dark eyes.

"I said no pictures." His voice sounded deeper than usual.

She cocked an eyebrow. "Uh, yeah, you said that. About three times. What's your hang-up?"

"Why do you care?"

"Because my job is to get the shot—"

He scoffed. "You got a shot. Of Grant. He's the pretty one, anyway. So can I leave now without being accosted again?"

She jerked her head back. "I'm *accosting* you?"

"You're preventing me from leaving."

"Why are you so angry?"

The words were said quick and on a shout. And they both recoiled, she as if surprised by her own words, and Ethan at the vehemence of her tone.

He wanted to point at the scars on his neck. He wanted to pull out the photo of his dead sister and shove it in her face. There were many, many reasons he was angry, but all of them he'd caused himself.

He stepped closer to her, but the minute he did, all rational thought seemed to leave his brain. She smelled amazing, like flowers and coconut, like a tropical paradise mirage. Up close, her brown eyes were wide and warm, ensnaring his gaze so he couldn't look away.

Her lips parted as she stared up at him, her chest rising and falling. Her cheeks were slightly redder than they'd been before. Was it possible she was as affected by him as he was by her?

As if she couldn't help herself, she closed the distance between them, so that their chests brushed, and he thought belatedly that he should step back. Get away. But before he could, she made a small gasping sound as the hard shaft in his pants brushed her stomach.

But she didn't step back. She didn't move at all. He could

reach out a hand and brush his fingers along the tops of her full breasts. He could bend down and take that gorgeous mouth, find out if she tasted as good as she looked.

He didn't even make a conscious effort to do it, and he hadn't realized that he had bent down, intent on pressing his lips to hers, until she inhaled sharply and stepped back, taking her scent with her, along with her warm eyes and those sweetly parted lips.

Her brown eyes flickered, her head dipped, so he couldn't see what those expressive eyes held.

Great, so now he'd sexually harassed the photographer. Before he got himself in further trouble, before he said or did something worse, he clamped his lips shut, shot her his best impassive expression, and nodded curtly.

Then he turned around, pushed the door open with an aggressive shove, and resisted all his instinct to catch one last glimpse of the enchanting Lissa Kingsman.

Chapter Two

Lissa finished editing the images of Grant and then fired them off in an email to Sal at the *Willow Park Daily*.

It was Monday, the day after the shoot at *Gamers*, and Lissa was in her photography studio on Main Street. She loved her little place in a strip mall that also had a grocery, a liquor store, and a gift shop.

Her finger hovered over the button of her mouse and she bit her lip, staring at her raw images folder. Just one peek. Her assistant was off getting lunch for them, so no one would know.

With a sharp intake of breath, she opened the folder and scrolled to the one image she'd managed to take—okay, steal—of Ethan Talley. He'd said no pictures and she'd honored that…kind of. She hadn't sent this picture to Sal to use, and Lissa now felt like a total creep, but she'd wanted a little something of the man who'd intrigued her.

In the picture, he was staring out the window. She'd snapped it when he wasn't paying attention, when he thought she was taking pictures of Grant, but she'd clicked the shutter when she dropped the camera to her side. He was in profile, the sun highlighting his face, his hands shoved deep in his pockets.

He'd been about to kiss her in the foyer at the *Gamers* office. And for a moment, she'd been about to let him. Something about his cold glare, his pained expression, his all black suit made her want to see what he'd be like warmed up. Hell, even with a smile.

She pressed a hand to her chest, her breath catching when she realized she hadn't seem him smile once.

Back when he was E-Rad, his smile was ever-present on his handsome face. She was sure he was rarely recognized, if ever. If it wasn't for his voice, which she knew so well, he probably wouldn't have seemed familiar at all.

There was a chasm, a whole lifetime, it seemed, between E-Rad and Ethan Talley.

She leaned closer, narrowing her eyes on the scars creeping up his neck. "What happened to you, Ethan?"

Would a kiss from her have brought a smile to his face? She wasn't so sure she had magical powers like that. Plus, she still wanted to find a way to get him to commit to her project. Getting involved romantically with him, while it sounded insanely hot, was unethical. Kissing him—and maybe more—was not the way to get him to agree to let her take his picture. She had principles, after all.

The bell over the front door chimed, and Lissa slid the image to a password-protected folder then closed out all of her windows.

Her assistant, Daniel Huang, dropped a Chipotle bag on her desk. "Here's your burrito bowl, Master."

She snatched it up and pulled out the container. "I told you not to call me that."

Daniel grinned and sank down onto a chair beside her, propping his feet on her desk. She pointed at the soles of his

Vans. "And I told you not to do that!"

He just shrugged and stuffed a taco in his mouth.

Her assistant was cheeky. But he was very organized—unlike her—and was excellent at making little children laugh so their parents were thrilled with their portraits, so she kept him around. He was a student at the local university but only took classes part-time. The rest of the time, he was hers to torture. "Thanks for getting lunch."

"No problem, I was hungry for guac. So did you manage to score pictures of that guy at the magazine?"

She pushed around the contents of her burrito bowl. "No, he was…resistant."

Daniel raised an eyebrow. "Resistant? And you couldn't charm your way into getting your lens on him?"

"I think he was charmed, but my lens was still not his friend." The memory of the heat of his body made her shiver.

"Bummer. So how's the project looking?"

She wiped her mouth and opened up her file for the Rona's Scars project.

Every time she photographed someone who was scarred and listened to their story, she came away bruised, but also fuller. After a car accident had left her sister, Rona, with severe scarring on her face and the use of only one eye, she'd begun to lose her ambitious drive that had always made her Rona. Lissa's big sister. Her idol.

She'd been studying to be a lawyer, and while Lissa and the rest of her family thought Rona was coping well, she wasn't. At all. And a year after the accident, she'd taken her own life with a bottle of pills.

The guilt over what she could have done to help her sister, how she could have prevented her death, was a constant weight on Lissa's shoulders, sometimes so heavy she couldn't breathe.

Starting the Rona's Scars project and the scholarship was

the only way she felt like she could give back. For the project, she talked to people who dealt with physical, non-genetic disabilities, and once the website launched, she hoped the pictures and stories would make others in similar situations feel less alone.

Donations would go to the scholarship fund, which would be awarded to black women studying to be lawyers.

This was her dream, her sole focus. And she'd roped Daniel into it, too.

She gazed at the list of participants. "We have about a dozen. I'd really like a couple more."

He nodded. "Too bad that guy was a bust."

Lissa bit her lip. As much as she wanted Ethan to sign on, she had a feeling dealing with him would be like walking on fire. "Yeah, I don't know what I'm going to do."

Daniel tossed his wrapper in the trash and stood up. "I'm going to get the studio ready. You have a family shoot in a half hour."

She waved him off and he strode out of the room, whistling to himself. Her cell phone rang, and she smiled when she saw who was calling. She answered it. "Hey."

"Hey, babe." Chad's voice was a little breathless, like he was running outside.

She frowned. "What're you doing?"

"We got a dog!"

She was in mid-sip of her soda and had to turn her head so she didn't spit it all over keyboard. "I'm sorry," she sputtered. "What did you say?"

"O and I got a dog. He's this tiny little yappy thing. We got him at the shelter, and he's mixed with, like, three breeds. He's actually kind of ugly, but O fell in love with him."

Chad, the former wild child who couldn't be tied down, had moved in with his boyfriend Owen and lately they were the perfect example of domestic bliss. Now, with a dog. "So why are you running?"

"Oh, I'm at the park and he pulled the leash out of my hands. I had to run after him."

"And you called me mid-chase?"

"I needed something to get my mind off the fact that I was running. It's all good now. Got the leash!"

She smiled. "You're weird."

His voice was muffled. "Don't do that, Dap!"

"Dap?"

His words were clearer now. "Yeah, Owen named him Dapper, and he wears a little bow tie. It's pretty fucking cute, honestly."

"I can't believe you have a dog. And a boyfriend."

His laugh was loud in her ear. "You and me both, babe. Anyway, what's up?"

"You called me."

"How'd that thing with Ethan go?"

She blew out a breath. "Oh, Chad."

He didn't speak for a minute. "Dude's kind of a brick wall."

"You think? He wouldn't even let me take pictures for the magazine. I didn't even bother to ask him about my project." A bell jingled from over the phone and then, a wet sound. "Chad?"

"Sorry." He grunted then said something muffled. "I picked up Dap and he attacked my face with his tongue. God, his breath smells. Anyway, Ethan'll be at Marley's wedding, you know."

Lissa straightened in her seat. The wedding was in two weeks, and she was the photographer for the event. "Seriously?"

"Yep. Rare for him to attend anything social, but he RSVP'd yes. You get another shot to charm him, babe."

She rubbed her sweaty palms on her pants. Why was she

so nervous now? All she had to do was talk to him again. Maybe he'd be less angry this time. Weddings were happy, right? He'd be happy. And maybe drunk. This could totally work in her favor. "Okay, this is good news. Maybe I can catch him alone at the end of the night."

Chad paused. "Alone?"

"You know what I—"

"Please don't tell me you found that grumpy bastard attractive."

She bit her lips.

"Jesus Christ," he muttered. "Ethan's, like, immune to happiness."

She thought about asking Chad what happened to him, why he didn't smile and had scars on his neck, but that felt violating. If she was going to do this, then she was going to give the guy the honor of letting him tell her his secrets. She shrugged, even though she knew Chad couldn't see her. "I don't know, I think the right person could make him happy."

Chad didn't speak for a minute, and when he did, his voice was softer. "I gotta go, babe, but just be careful, okay? You've been through a lot and you're still shining like a diamond. I don't want anyone to dull that."

Her eyes stung as she said her good-byes to her friend and hung up the phone. She glanced at the clock and wiped under her cheeks, because her clients were going to be here in ten minutes.

She didn't want to dull her shine, either, but she would have loved to share it with someone, if it was needed. And if anyone needed a little shine in his life, it was Ethan Talley.

• • •

Ethan didn't understand what was wrong with his black suit.

His sister Chloe wasn't so bashful anymore, not since she

hooked up with Grant. She didn't tiptoe around Ethan, and while he'd been glad about it at first, this bold Chloe was into "fixing" him.

He didn't need to be fixed.

The main reason was there were no broken pieces anymore. They'd been crushed long ago. Ethan was quite whole; there just wasn't much to him anymore.

Chloe tapped her finger to her chin and held up a series of ties she'd brought over. "These will all match the wedding party. Do you like any of them?"

He eyed the pile of silk. "What's wrong with my black-and-white-striped tie?"

"Which one?" She flailed an arm toward his closet at his tie rack, which held…okay, a lot of black and white ties.

He didn't answer, and she rolled her eyes. "Please, for the love of God, let's get some color on you."

"I wear color sometimes," he pointed out.

"Yes, but this is a wedding. You're supposed to look festive."

He sighed and leaned back against the wall, his arms crossed over his gray T-shirt. "You pick."

She looked at the ties, running her fingers down a couple before she settled on a plain pale blue tie. She held it up to his face and smiled. "This one."

He took it from her and rubbed it between his fingers. To be fair, it was a great tie. "Why this one?"

"It looks nice with your eyes."

Hers were filling now, and fuck, was she going to cry? He tugged her to him in a brief hug then let her go, refusing to look into her face, because that might start a discussion about him. He didn't want to talk about himself. "So I'll wear this one. Anything else?"

He heard a small sniffle and then her voice, which was clearer than he expected. "I have a blue handkerchief to match. For your pocket."

He turned around and held out his hand for the fabric square. "Thank you." She nodded then gathered up the ties and stuck them in the bag she brought to return the ones he didn't want. "I really appreciate it."

She looked up, and yes, her eyes were wet. "I know this wedding isn't on your list of things you'd like to do, but it means a lot to me that you'll be there. And Grant. You are a part of this whole family, you know?"

The word family made him cringe. Their family was broken. "Right." His voice sounded hoarse.

Chloe flinched. "Ethan—"

"Of course I'll be at the wedding. I've gotten to know Austin and Marley more since I took over *Gamers*, and I want to be there for them." But he didn't want to be told he was part of a family. The only family he cared about was Chloe, his youngest sister. The sibling who was still alive. His best friend, really.

Her struggle over the death of their sister still cut him to the core, as if he'd been hollowed out with a serrated knife. But she'd found happiness now, with the ever-happy Grant and his teenage daughter. They'd kept their relationship a secret from him at first because they worried about how protective he was over his sister, and that made him feel worse. He wanted Chloe to be able to share the joys of her life with him. She wasn't meant to be in the muck where he was stuck.

She stepped closer to him, the bag in her hand. "I have to go, but do you want to come over tonight? Sydney's cooking."

That was the only way to get him out of his house other than work. Grant's daughter was a teenage baking machine. But he wasn't in the mood tonight. He smiled at his sister. "I appreciate it, but I'm staying in tonight."

She widened her eyes in mock surprise. "Staying in, huh?

Wow, mixing it up for once."

He shoved her shoulder gently. "Shut up."

She rolled her eyes. "Fine, but if you change your mind, give me a call."

"Will do. Thanks for the ties."

He saw his sister out and then headed to the home gym in his basement. He pushed himself hard on the weight bench, doing bench presses. Then he ran on his treadmill for longer than he should have. After a shower to clean off the smell of sweat and iron, he heated up some leftover lasagna and parked himself in front of the TV.

He used to work out because he cared about how he looked. That his abs were defined, his pecs even, his shoulders round.

Now, he worked out because it was the one way he could punish himself physically. He upped his weights until he shook and ran on the treadmill until he almost passed out. It was one of the reasons Chloe brought him so much food. He'd lost weight in the last couple of years.

Although, he'd spent a little time in front of the mirror today—which was rare. He didn't look at his face, but he'd studied his muscles a little, flexing his arms. He tried to look at himself through, say, that photographer's eyes. Was he anything worth looking at anymore?

And then he felt like a tool, so he'd gotten in the shower and didn't look in the mirror again.

On nights like this, he wondered what his parents were doing. MLB playoffs were on, and he could imagine his dad on his recliner, beer bottle in hand, a bowl of peanuts on the table beside him. Just like always.

Ethan had once been welcome there.

But not anymore. And he knew it was all his doing. Chloe insisted he could make up with their parents, but it'd been so long and the hurt ran so deep, like scarred skin that hadn't been stitched properly. It'd never be the same or smooth again. There'd always be a divide.

He hated that his sister had placed the weight of trying to mend their family on her shoulders, but now that she no longer thought of it as her job, she was much happier.

And Ethan *was* happy, because she was happy.

He only wished he could say the same for himself. Instead, he sat eating leftover lasagna, missing his family, and dreading attending a wedding.

Oh, and he still couldn't get the sight of that photographer's big brown eyes out of his head.

Chapter Three

Ethan slid into an empty seat in the last row right as the music changed from a bland melody to the opening notes of Pachelbel's Canon.

He straightened his blue tie and nodded at his sister, who caught his eye from five rows in front of him. She raised an eyebrow and shook her head, and he quirked his lips. Hey, no one said he had to be early.

He shifted in his seat and thumbed the program. In gray cursive it announced the marriage of Austin Rivers and Marley Lake. A light breeze blew among the gathered guests as the first bridesmaid walked down the aisle. Ethan craned his head and watched as Sydney held her bouquet out in front of her, smiling as she made her way to the end of the aisle, where Austin stood, along with Grant and Chad—Marley's brother. The wedding was being held at a local park, and the fall leaves created a crunchy carpet under their feet.

Next was a woman Ethan didn't recognize, but the program told him she was Marley's cousin.

The music paused and then started up again as Marley

came into view, striding across the park with an older man holding her arm. The guests stood up and cameras snapped. Tissues were pulled out as tears started. Ethan remained unmoved, yet he had to admit Marley looked gorgeous.

When the congregation sat down, Ethan eyed Austin, who watched his bride with wet eyes.

Ethan ducked his head as the naked emotion on the otherwise stoic Austin tightened his chest. Through his lashes, he looked at the back of Chloe's head, and fisted his hand on his leg as she raised a tissue to the corner of her eye.

This would be her soon, he was sure. Grant would ask her to marry him. There'd be family events and a wedding, but Ethan knew the whole time, there would be a huge, gaping hole where Samantha should have been. His parents would give him the cold shoulder, because they didn't talk to him anymore, not since Samantha passed.

He squeezed his eyes shut as he thought of his sister and took deep breaths so he didn't lose his shit at the wedding. It'd been close to ten years, but he still felt nauseous when he thought of her. The last image he had of her flashed through his brain—her laughing face right before he took a corner too tight in his flashy car, wanting to show off. And then her wide eyes, her open mouth, as soon as she realized he'd lost control of the car.

After the crash, when he finally gained consciousness, she wasn't alive, and his skin refused to let him forget it.

Forget that he'd driven the car that caused the death of the beautiful, charming, full-of-light Samantha Talley.

Fuck, he was getting somber again. He took a deep breath and opened his eyes, only to stare into the warm brown ones of Lissa Kingsman.

She stood alongside the chairs, wearing a long black dress, her camera clutched in her hand with a zoom lens.

Her gaze on him was like a shot of whiskey, a searing

heat that spread out to all his limbs, warming him to the core. Her lips parted slightly, and her full lashes fluttered. Then she dipped her chin once in acknowledgement, quirking her lips in a half smile, and then turned away, raising her camera up to her eye to take pictures of the ceremony.

Ethan focused on his breathing—namely, making sure he was breathing—and trying not to read too much into that small smile.

It wasn't even a full one. *Get a fucking grip.*

He hated that she stirred these…feelings in him. That she made him give a shit that she smiled rather than sneered after the way he'd treated her.

That she made him a little hard.

He spent the rest of the ceremony watching her as discretely as he could, admiring the fluidity of her movements, the way her tongue snuck out the corner of her mouth when she concentrated, and the way her large hoop earrings caught the light of the sun setting behind them.

When the ceremony was over, he was one of the first out of his seats, striding toward the parking lot where he could spend some time alone in his car before having to face everyone at the reception.

Except he heard his name being called. By the very woman he never said no to. So he checked his expression to make sure he didn't look stressed or panicked and turned around to face his sister.

Chloe was jogging toward him, her heels sinking a little in the grass. He held out a hand. "Slow down. You're going to trip."

She laughed as she wobbled. "The ground's soft."

"It just rained. Now walk, please, before I carry you."

She rolled her eyes and came to a stop in front of him. Running a hand down his tie, she gazed up. "You look so nice."

"And you look beautiful, Chloe." She wore a slim-fitting

dark blue dress that came down to just below her knee.

With a smirk, she jutted a hip out. "You think."

"I *know*."

She smiled and slipped her arm in his. "I need a ride to the reception. Grant's going in the limo. They said I could come, but I told them I wanted to go with you."

He bristled. That was just like Chloe to think her poor, scarred brother needed a companion. "I don't need a babysitter."

She frowned. "I didn't say you did. *I* want to ride with you."

Well, now he felt stupid. "Oh."

When they reached his car, he opened the door for her and she stepped inside. He shut it behind her, and as he walked around the front of his car, jingling his keys, he spotted Lissa standing near a tree, studying the back of her camera. Her head was bent down, hair framing her face.

There was a knocking sound, and he turned around to see Chloe looking at him with her hands out to the sides. Shit, he'd stopped walking and stared at Lissa like a weirdo. Chloe probably thought he was crazy. He ducked his head and resumed his way around his car. When he settled himself in the driver's seat, Chloe was craning her neck to peer through the windshield. "What were you looking at?"

"Uh, just a squirrel."

She turned her head slowly. "A squirrel."

"Ah, yup."

"You were not looking at a squirrel. You were frozen in place, captivated by something, and it sure as hell wasn't a squirrel. You hate squirrels!"

That was true. He did hate squirrels. They threw acorns. "Okay, fine, I was looking at the photographer."

He was pulling out of the parking lot now, but that didn't stop Chloe from twisting in her seat to stare out the back window. "The photographer? Why? Did you know him?"

Him? There must have been two photographers. Well, that sure helped him. "Uh, I thought he looked familiar is all."

"Oh," Chloe said, clearly disappointed there wasn't something juicy to the whole thing.

He snorted. "Sorry it wasn't more exciting."

"I'm living with Grant. I have enough excitement in my life."

Ethan chuckled under his breath. "Yeah, I'm sure."

"Save a dance for me at the reception, okay?"

He patted her knee. "'Course."

Three hours later, Ethan took a swallow of bourbon and tried not to scowl at all the happy couples at the wedding reception.

Marley and Austin were at the newlywed table, feeding each other cake. Grant was singing off-key to a giggling Chloe on the dance floor, and Chad was eating his boyfriend's face in their seats about five feet away.

Ethan was alone, which was on purpose. He was happy that way. Until today, of course. Surrounded by love and family.

Earlier, he'd seen Lissa with another photographer, though that man had long since left. She was finished taking photos, her camera bag under guard by Owen as she pulled a laughing Chad onto the dance floor.

Her body moved like water, every movement fluid and purposeful and controlled. Her hips rolled against Chad's, her long arms wrapped around his shoulders. He pressed a kiss to her neck and she laughed.

Grant had told Ethan earlier that Chad and Lissa were friends, and even though Chad was committed to Owen, Ethan couldn't help the surge of jealousy that left a sour taste in his mouth.

As the song changed to something slower and more sultry, Ethan willed himself to stay in his seat, told himself to stay put, but his body wasn't listening—and neither was his cock, for that matter. He strode onto the dance floor, his dress shoes clicking on the tile floor. Chad was whispering something in Lissa's ear as Ethan approached.

"Excuse me," he all but growled.

Chad's head lifted and Lissa turned to stare at him in surprise. Ethan lifted her hand from Chad's shoulder and tugged her to him, where she smashed against his chest with an *oomph*. Ethan gazed into those deep brown eyes. "I believe you owe me a dance."

She blinked at him, those impossibly thick lashes fluttering. "Uh, I'm pretty sure we never talked about a dance. You must be mistaking me for someone else."

He held firm as she tugged to get out of his grip. "I'd like to dance with you. Please."

So he was a little rusty. A lot rusty. Chad looked at him like he was an alien before turning to Lissa. "You all right?"

She hesitated then nodded. "Sure. Watch my camera?"

"Of course." With one last look over his shoulder, Chad left the dance floor.

Lissa peered up at him. "Are you asking me to dance with you?"

"Will you say yes?"

She smiled at that. "Ask me and find out."

He licked his lips, wishing he could bend down and nibble on her plump ones. "Will you dance with me?"

She cocked her head, long gold earrings brushing her neck. "Yes."

He wrapped both arms around her, resting his hands on her lower back. He didn't go lower, no matter how much he wanted to grab a handful of her ass.

Tone it down, man, you're acting crazy.

But her touch was only fueling this unusual surge of desperate *want* inside him. She rested one hand on his hip, the other clasped around his neck, long fingernails digging into his nape. He was hard, again, and there was no way she didn't feel it. Her body was smooth and pliant under his hands. The low-cut neckline of her dress showed him the tops of her round, full breasts. He wanted to bury his face in her cleavage as he drove into her.

Oh fuck, he was getting harder.

He would have been embarrassed if it wasn't for the way Lissa was responding.

Her hands tightened where she held him, and her lips were parted as their groins pressed together. She looked up at him, her cheeks flushed a deep red. She was affected, too—she had to be. He was surprised as hell this woman seemed to want his grumpy, deformed self, but he wasn't sure he'd be able to think of anything else until he had her.

He'd been good at this once. Cocky and self-assured and confident, he'd been able to talk a woman into his bed and then keep her there with his skills. He used to be quite excellent with his mouth. In all things.

He leaned down and took a chance, figuring if she smacked him, he wouldn't have lost anything. His hand drifted lower until his fingers skimmed the top of her ass. He squeezed, and her breath caught as she pressed closer. He welcomed the pain of her nails digging into his neck.

He leaned down until his lips were at her ear. "I want you." She made a small sound in her throat, but she didn't move away. That was encouraging. "I have since I saw you in my office. Do you want me, Lissa?"

She nodded so slightly he thought maybe he imagined it.

"I need you to say it out loud."

She leaned back so she met his gaze and licked her lips.

"Yes."

He bent his head so all he saw were her eyes. "This isn't a date," he said firmly, knowing he was coming across harsh, but he was too old and too damaged to deal with bullshit. "I don't want to chitchat and meet your parents. I want *inside* you."

She wasn't shocked by his words. The only indication she had heard him was a slight dilation of her pupils and her heart pounding against his.

And then he waited, unsure if she'd leave him aching and hard or if she'd follow through with what they both clearly wanted to do.

Chapter Four

Lissa was about two seconds away from shoving Ethan onto his back on the dance floor and riding him like a fucking bull.

She'd dated a lot of men who weren't up front, who acted like they wanted a girlfriend when they really just wanted a fuck.

She wasn't opposed to just a fuck. But she didn't like being lied to. Ethan was a little cold and a lot vulgar, but he was honest.

Her mind told her to walk away. To tell him that she didn't want him, that she didn't want this. Sleeping with Ethan would put a serious crimp in her plans to invite him to participate in her project. She didn't want him thinking that she'd only slept with him to get him to agree. This wasn't the time to spring it on him, though. And right now, her brain was clouded with lust; her body's only objective was to get this man alone. His hard cock was pressed against her, and his words were ringing in her ear.

It'd been a long time since she'd had a man between her legs; she'd been so busy with work and with her project. Would it really hurt to use him just like he wanted to use her? It was only one time, and he'd pursued her. It couldn't hurt, right?

She swallowed. "So it's just sex?"

He nodded. "Just sex."

Oh fuck, she wanted that. She wanted this big man's dick in her hand, in her body. She was wet already just from the words he'd whispered in her ear. Her favorite type of foreplay was to get hot and bothered in public and then rush off somewhere private to get naked.

She pressed closer to Ethan, trapping his hard cock between them. His jaw clenched, and she shot him what she hoped was a sexy smile. "You want to fuck me, Ethan?" He sucked in a breath and his hand drifted lower until he was kneading one cheek of her ass. Her nipples tightened as a ripple of arousal coursed through her body. "You're so hard. I'd bet you'd fuck me so good, wouldn't you? Bend me over a table and pull my dress up. Rip off these tiny panties I have on and punish me for making you want this much."

She was poking the beast. Ethan's other hand was on her neck now, his thumb stroking over the tendon. "If you don't stop with that mouth, I'll fuck you right here in front of God and everyone."

She was a raging mass of hormones with no brain. "I dare you."

With a soft growl, Ethan gripped her hand and all but dragged her from the dance floor. She trotted after him, thankful the lights were dim and everyone else was too drunk to notice. She didn't know where they were going, but Ethan powered out the doors of the reception hall and strode toward the front lobby. He stopped in front of the bathrooms and said, "Stay right here," and she was too turned on to protest that he'd just given her a command like she was a disobedient puppy.

He disappeared into the men's room and in ten seconds,

he was back out again, clutching a condom packet. Her breath sped up and her heart pounded so loudly she heard it in her ears.

He glanced at the front doors before muttering "fuck it" under his breath and pushing through a door in front of them marked COAT CLOSET.

With only a dim light shining overhead, he pressed her along the back wall, among coats and fake furs and trenches. She gripped a suit jacket, needing something to ground her as his body pressed along hers.

His mouth descended and then he was kissing her. All tongue and teeth and want. She moaned into his mouth and clutched his shoulders as he hiked her leg over his hip. His other hand scrabbled to get under her dress and then he pulled away from her mouth with a growl and looked down their bodies. "What's with this fucking dress? I want to touch you, dammit."

She reached down, pulled up her dress to expose the small black thong she was wearing, and bared her teeth at him. "Then touch me."

As if he wanted to punish her for the fabric she'd draped over her body, he lunged at her, biting her bare shoulder. She couldn't stop the whimper that escaped, which morphed into a moan as he wasted no time tugging aside her thong and plunging two fingers inside of her.

He bit harder, and her eyes fell closed as his hand stilled. The only sound was the panting of her breath, the harsh gasps where he sought to breathe around her skin. He unlocked his jaw and when he lifted his head, the dim light of the ceiling cast a shadow under his eyes. His lips curled, almost into a sneer, as he slowly drew his fingers out and then pushed them back in. The force drew her up onto the ball of her foot, as her other leg was still hiked over his hip, his hand trapped between them as his fingers began a steady rhythm.

With his other hand, he massaged her thigh, keeping her spread open against the wall.

For a split second, she thought she should stop this. Tell him to take her home. They were in a coat closet, where anyone could come in.

But then his hand twisted and his thumb pressed against her clit and she had to shove her hand in her mouth to keep from screaming.

He shook his head as he continued to torture her. "I want to hear you."

"I'm loud."

"Good. Scream for me."

He pulled down the neck of her dress so one of her breasts popped out, and while his fingers drove her mad, he sucked a nipple into the wet heat of his mouth.

She cried out as he bit down, rolling the hard bud between his teeth. "Oh fuck, oh fuck," she chanted, the sensation on her breasts echoing in the constant pressure of his thumb against her clit.

He nuzzled in, lapping at her breast, and taking one small nip before he leaned back with a satisfied smirk on his face. "You look debauched." His voice was a low rumble. "Breast out, legs spread open, my fingers inside of you."

She was close now, and while one hand clutched his shoulder, she needed something else, something that wasn't him to remind her what this was about. Her fingers clutched a wool jacket and the scratchy fiber tickled her palm.

"Say my name when you come, Lissa."

She nodded mutely. She understood, but she wasn't sure if she was going to be able, because she couldn't find words right now.

"Fucking beautiful," he muttered, his gaze cast down where his hand was between her legs. "I love the way you move when you're so close to coming."

And that did it, with a cry and a gasp that she hoped sounded something like his name, she came. The orgasm rippled through her, out to her limbs and into the tips of her fingers. Her inner walls clenched around his thick fingers, and he didn't take his eyes off her the whole time.

Before the aftershocks of the orgasm ended, Ethan spun her around. She found herself braced against the wall, bent over. She curled her fingers into the wall and pressed her cheek between them.

Cool air touched her ass and then fingertips skimmed along the edge of her thong. A palm smoothed over one cheek, then the other.

She knew she had a great ass. She got it from her momma, and she smiled as she heard him murmur in appreciation. A hand came down and cracked against her skin. She moaned and wiggled her ass, loving the sting. "You punishing me for making you hard, baby?" she asked. A smack to her other cheek, and she smiled. "Show me what you do to bad girls who make your cock ache."

The condom wrapper crinkled, and then the empty packet fluttered to the ground at their feet. After a minute, a hand reached around to squeeze her exposed breast, and then her dress was pulled lower so both breasts swung free.

He held them both in his palms, thumbing the nipples. The blunt head of his cock nudged her entrance. She wanted to see it, hold it in her palm, but this wasn't about that. This was an impersonal fuck. And she wanted it so goddamn bad.

"Well?" she challenged. "You said—"

His hands still on her breasts, he slammed into her so hard, the air left her body. She wished she could have seen that, the power and skill in his hips to enter her without a hand guiding his cock.

"I know what I said," he growled into her ear as he lay over her back. "I said I'd take your breath away. Did I do that?

Baby?" He punctuated the last word with a thrust of his hips.

She swallowed and worked on breathing so she could get her voice back. "Yes. Now fuck me good, because I'm supposed to come again, right?"

She loved his growl, loved how primal it was, how angry he got that she made him this turned on. "Oh you'll come again." He said it like a threat, like she wouldn't enjoy it.

"I'm holding you to it." She gritted her teeth as he slammed in again, his cock long and thick enough that it was touching places inside of her that rarely got any attention.

He began to fuck her with a rhythm she hadn't realized he possessed—careful rolls of his hips. While one hand teased a nipple, he skimmed the other hand down to slide into her wet folds. He focused on her engorged clit, rolling it between his fingertips until she could feel the beginning of another orgasm in the base of her spine. She wasn't sure she'd get there, but as if Ethan knew, he began to speed up his thrusts and kicked in more power behind them until he was pounding into her.

His body blanketed her back, and his lips were at her ear. "Fuck, you feel good. You knew I wanted you from the beginning, didn't you?"

She couldn't talk anymore, not while Ethan filled her to the brim, and those fingers were touching the areas on her body that were her most sensitive. "You knew, and you still flaunted that body in front of me, making me hurt. Who hurts now? Huh?"

"Me," she gasped out.

"That's right," he hissed, then bit down on her earlobe.

She came apart again, this orgasm leaving her a trembling, moaning mess as Ethan cursed behind her. His rhythm stuttered, his hands gripping her hips as he slammed into her one more time and roared.

Ethan's hands on her body were the only reason Lissa was still standing, because she wanted to crumble onto the ground in a pile of sex-sated bliss.

The man who'd just taken her to O-town twice—as he'd promised—hadn't moved from her body. He was still buried inside her, and as her muscles half-heartedly squeezed him, he sucked in a breath and slowly pulled out.

Lissa closed her eyes, wanting him to leave so they didn't have to go through awkward chitchat.

But he didn't move, the heat of his body still behind her.

. . .

Ethan didn't want to leave. Well he did, but then he didn't. Because Lissa was still here, her scent surrounding him like paradise.

He'd set the rules. This was it. Except he wanted to do it again. Fucking her had been the first time he'd felt alive in years.

He righted her dress, pulled the fabric down to cover the smooth, dark skin he wanted to touch again. He disposed of the condom and righted his clothes as best he could in the dim light.

He should probably say something, apologize for fucking her in a dark closet like a cave man. The absence of light had been the reason he'd been able to be this forward, but now, he worried it made him look like he was…embarrassed to be seen with her. Which was far from the truth. She should have been embarrassed to be seen with him.

She turned around, shimmying herself back into her dress. Her head was down and he wanted to say something, anything, which would make her know he wished he wasn't like this. "I'm sorry," he blurted out.

Her head shot up, her pupils so large her eyes looked nearly black. Her lips parted. "Excuse me?"

"I'm sorry…" He gestured toward their less-than-romantic setting. "For dragging you into a closet and—"

She held up a hand, silencing him. "You're apologizing?"

"Um—"

"Did you enjoy that?"

His mouth dropped open, and he shut it with a clack before licking his lips and trying for words. "Of course I enjoyed it. Your body is like heaven, and you smell like it, too." How was that for honesty?

Her head jolted, like she hadn't expected that, then her lips slowly quirked into a smile. "I enjoyed it, too. That was hot as hell, you wanting me so badly you couldn't wait to get me into a bed. And you're apologizing?"

"I wasn't sure—"

"You made it clear you wanted to fuck. And I agreed. So don't treat me like I'm some fragile thing who needs rose petals and cuddling now, okay?"

She was perfect. Every fucking inch of her, from those expressive eyes to the words that came out from between her lips. "Your mouth turns me on."

He'd lost a filter sometime in the last couple of years. Her eyebrows shot up and then she threw back her head and laughed, the sound like waves crashing and sun shining and everything happy. For a moment he forgot they were stuffed in a coat closet that smelled like sex. There was only her, and that laugh, and paradise.

When she lowered her gaze, her breath caught a moment as she studied his face.

"Why are you looking at me like that?" He touched his cheek, heat creeping up his neck. Was she going to ask about his scars? Because—

"You're smiling." Her voice was soft.

His hand traveled over his skin to touch his lips, and to his surprise, he *was* smiling. A real smile that he hadn't had to think about. When was the last time that had happened?

Lissa dug into the folds of her dress where she pulled a card from a hidden pocket he hadn't realized was there. She stared at it for a minute then took a deep breath before handing it to him. "Here."

He took the card and peered down at it, but he couldn't make out all the words in the dim light. "What's this?"

She smoothed her dress down. "My business card. If you ever want to fuck in a coat closet or a bed or desk or whatever, and maybe if you want to flash me that handsome smile again, give me a call. Cell phone number is on the back."

She brushed past him, their shoulders touching for an instant. He was still staring at the card when she called his name. He turned around to where she stood in the open doorway, the light from the hallway backlighting her hourglass figure. "Ethan?"

"Yes." His voice was hoarse.

Her eyes flashed. "I'll wear a shorter dress next time."

And then she was gone in a swirl of fabric.

Chapter Five

With her hands full of wine bottles and a cheese plate, Lissa kicked the door to her parents' house and waited impatiently. When the door didn't immediately open, she started yelling, too.

Her mother flung open the door when Lissa was mid-holler and glared. "Will you stop the racket, Lis? Goodness gracious. The neighbors are probably looking out their windows." She made a face at the house across the street. "The curtain moved. You know Old Man Grandy is tut-tutting about my loud children."

As the middle child growing up, Lissa had to be extra loud to get attention. That trait hadn't quite worn off yet. She assumed it never would. She smacked a kiss on her mom's cheek. "Who cares what Old Man Grandy thinks?"

Her mom huffed but wrapped Lissa in a hug, jabbing one of the bottles into her ribs. "Okay, maybe not so tight on the hug."

Her mom leaned back and patted her face. "You look beautiful as always."

"Good genes, I guess." Lissa handed her mom the wine and

then followed her into the kitchen. The greatest compliment she could ever get was when people said she looked like her mother. Ariel Kingsman was a stunning woman. Mahogany skin and big brown eyes. High cheekbones that rivaled Iman's.

Her younger brother, Angel, was already in the kitchen, drinking a beer with their father. Lissa kissed them both then set the cheese plate on the counter. She and Angel were born less than a year apart, so they'd always been close, the two troublemakers who'd had a safety net consisting of their parents and Rona. There was an irreparable hole in that safety net now, leaving her and Angel to cling to each other even more. They even shared an apartment.

Her mother interrupted her thoughts by holding out a glass of wine. Dinner was their regular Sunday routine. Sometimes one or more of them had to miss a meal, but they tried to make every Sunday they could.

This house would always be home to Lissa. There was the living room where she'd played video games with Angel, the kitchen where she'd baked cookies with Rona, and the bedroom where she'd lie awake at night, dreaming about being a famous wildlife photographer. At least she'd gotten one half of that dream. Although attempting to photograph Ethan Talley was a little like dealing with a pissed-off lion.

Stop thinking about him and that damn coat closet.

She plastered on a smile and took the wine glass from her mom, who shot her a look. Lissa turned away quickly before her mom saw her fake smile and called her on it.

"What's going on?"

Oh shit, too late. *Moms.*

Lissa took a gulp of her wine and turned back around to see all three family members staring at her. "What?"

Angel cocked his head. "You kinda went somewhere for a minute."

"Yeah, I did. In my own head."

"Wanna share?"

"No, I do not. It's nice and private in there." She huffed. "We live together, and you never knock on my bedroom door. I'm not letting you in my head, too."

Angel opened his mouth to backtalk, she was sure, but Lissa's mother interrupted. "Enough. Both of you. How you live together is a mystery to me."

"We grew up together. We're related. Brother and sister." Angel took a sip of his beer then grinned innocently.

His mom smacked him. "All of you, leave. I need to finish getting dinner ready."

"Need help?" Lissa asked.

Her mom answered her by shooing her out of the kitchen.

Lissa, Angel, and their father retreated to the living room, where they watched baseball and devoured the cheese tray.

Her father watched her over the rim of his glasses. Carl Kingsman was a serious man, in sharp contrast to their loud, gregarious mother. And after Rona's death, he smiled even less. The absence of laugh lines around his mouth hurt Lissa's heart.

"Have you formed the committee to review the scholarship applications?"

That was her dad. He worried about the details. While Lissa had her head in the clouds, daydreaming about the photos and the project, her father kept her on task regarding the business side of her project. "Yeah, some of Lissa's grad school friends, as well as some professors from her alma mater."

Her father nodded. "Good. Rona would be pleased."

Lissa picked at a rip in her jeans. She hoped so. Growing up as a black American, it'd been evident to them from the very beginning that they had to work extra hard to have less than what someone with lighter skin would have. Rona had been determined to be the best lawyer she could be, to fight for those who didn't have anyone else fighting for them. She was proud of her skin, her heritage, and everything that she'd worked for.

After talking with her family, Lissa decided supporting young women like Rona, with the same ambitions, would be the best way to honor her sister. She wanted Rona to be remembered for how she'd lived, not how she'd died.

But no matter how hard she tried, it was nearly impossible to sum up Rona's life. Lissa couldn't show everyone the red stain on her bedroom carpet, where they'd spilled nail polish at night when they were supposed to be sleeping. She couldn't point to the corner of the basement, where Rona would model dress-up clothes, and Lissa found her love of photography by taking pictures of her. She couldn't recreate Rona's laugh—which was sometimes hyena-like.

So this project was the only way she knew how, and it'd been her sole focus during the last year.

Lissa looked up when her father spoke again, but this time, his attention was on Angel. "And how's work?"

Angel was a manager at the Foot Locker in the mall, which was great, since he never wore the same shoes twice. He said he loved retail, but Lissa knew he had dreams of opening up his own restaurant. He tried to say cooking was just a hobby, but Lissa wasn't buying it.

Angel picked at his beer label. "Good. I hired a new assistant, and she's working out really well. In fact"—he grinned—"I think she might take my job if I'm not careful. Gotta step up my game."

Their father looked like he was going to ask more questions, but then he just nodded. "Well then, step it up."

Angel looked at Lissa and rounded his lips into an O, wiping imaginary sweat off of his face. She held back a smile.

Lissa leaned back, enjoying the comfortable silence that could only be achieved around family, and sipped her wine.

She hadn't told Angel yet about Ethan, even though she'd

been so tempted. But it all seemed like a dream now, what happened at the wedding. She knew he'd never call again, not surly Ethan.

But that didn't stop her from wondering about his story. There was a huge gap in his life, where he went from E-Rad to Ethan Talley, and not only was she curious, but she also couldn't stop thinking about the way he kissed her.

She was so distracted that she looked up to see her entire family staring at her. Again. "Oh jeez, what now?" she asked.

"I've been saying your name for a good thirty seconds to tell you dinner is ready." Her mom cocked out a hip. "Can we interrupt your daydream?"

She pursed her lips and stood up in a huff. "Busybody family members," she muttered under her breath as she walked by them.

"We heard that!" Angel called after her.

Lissa finished off her wine before setting the empty glass on the table. She really needed to get her head together, focus on her project, and forget about Ethan E-Rad Talley.

• • •

Ethan blinked at the kid—he refused to call this person a man—and waited for the next ridiculous thing to come out of his mouth.

As soon as Alex Hershel walked into his office, he knew this wasn't the man they wanted as the face of *Gamers*. He snapped his gum repeatedly, and his clothes were sloppy, styled in a way that was clearly on purpose and which Ethan felt was unprofessional.

The guy hadn't dropped the cocky grin, either. Ethan wasn't legally allowed to ask how old he was in a job interview, but he would place Alex somewhere around twenty-three. Maybe.

And everyone knew a man's brain didn't reach adulthood until twenty-five. Ethan had ruined his life before he hit twenty-five. He should know.

He stared down at the kid's resume, which used some funky font and colors, for God's sake. He wanted to explain that Times New Roman was classic, not old-fashioned.

"So." Alex cracked his gum, which was an unnatural yellow color. "What do you think?"

Ethan gazed at him levelly. "I think no."

The kid's expression faltered for the first time in a half hour. "What?"

"I'm sorry." Ethan handed him his resume. "But you're not what we're looking for."

Alex stared at his resume then at Ethan. "Really?"

Ethan flared his nostrils and counted to five so he wouldn't blow his lid. "Yes, really."

"Huh." Alex reached out and took his resume, then stared at it as if it held the answer to his future. "Have any advice for me for future interviews?"

Didn't they mentor kids these days anymore? "Yes, next time, wear a suit, get rid of the gum, and apply for a job you're qualified for."

A low whistle made them both look up. Grant leaned on the doorframe of Ethan's office, his hands in his pockets. "Way harsh, Talley."

Alex just stared at him, and Ethan snorted softly. *Clueless* was probably released before this guy was born.

Grant sauntered forward after shooting a glare at Ethan. "Excuse my partner here. He's a little grumpy today. Just like every day. I'm Grant Osprey."

Alex shifted his gaze to Ethan and then back to Grant like he was the second coming. "Alex Hershel."

"He was just leaving," Ethan prodded.

Grant took Alex's résumé out of his hands and smiled at

him. "I'll take a look at this, and we'll call you if we want to speak to you further."

"Don't give him false hope, Grant," Ethan said.

His friend widened his eyes at him. "Can you cool it?"

Ethan pressed his lips together.

Alex's gaze was ping-ponging between the two of him, and he was half sitting, half standing in his chair, like he didn't know whether to stay or go. Ethan was done with this interview, with the day, with the whole fucking week. Grant must have sensed his frustration was reaching a boiling point, because he led Alex out of the office and shook his hand at the door, sending him on his way.

Ethan bent forward until his forehead rested on the smooth wood of his desk. He breathed out, and stayed that way until the squeak of the leather chair across from him and a throat clearing let him know Grant was still there.

"You all right?"

Ethan lifted his head and rubbed his forehead. "Yeah."

"You look stressed."

"I *am* stressed. We want to get a decision made on the host for our channel, and no one I've had in here is fit for the job. The closest we had was that former gaming champ, but she's not interested anymore."

Grant was silent.

"Why aren't you saying words?" Ethan frowned. "You're always talking. That's what you *do*."

"What's with you lately?" Grant asked. "You've been like this since Austin's wedding."

Great, now they were analyzing him. "You said I'm always grumpy, so what's the difference?"

Grant shook his head. "Sure, you're usually grumpy, but in an…expressionless way. Now it's like all of a sudden you're frustrated and stressed and actually pissed off about something."

Ethan scowled. "I am not pissed off."

Grant raised his eyebrows.

This was getting old. "This conversation is over."

Grant sighed. "Look, you want to know what I think about this whole host search?"

Ethan threw up his hands. "Yes, I'd love to know. We're partners in this, so—"

Grant jumped up and leaned over Ethan's desk, his hands braced on the front. "I think the search is fucking dumb!"

Ethan fell back in his chair and looked up at his usually amicable friend. He rarely heard Grant raise his voice. "I'm sorry? I thought you agreed we needed a host—"

Grant met his gaze steadily. "I do think we need a host, Ethan. The problem is that I think we need to be looking in-house."

Ethan let his gaze slip to his door, where he caught glimpses of some of their staff. "Oh, well then who? Has someone expressed interest?"

"You're such a dumb fuck."

Ethan snapped his gaze to Grant. "I think the name-calling is unnecessary."

"I'm talking about you," Grant said, his tone deceptively quiet. "You know how to talk on camera, how to appeal to our target audience. You made millions doing it once. You could do it again, you know."

It was like Grant had dumped a bucket of ice on Ethan's head. His entire body was frozen solid, like his fingers would crack in half if he bent them. He'd thought Grant understood him. He'd thought Grant was his friend, but he wasn't so sure anymore, not if he didn't understand why asking Ethan to go on camera again was like sending him to hell.

He wanted to throw something, or hit something, so it took all his strength to sit motionless and say, "Please leave my office now."

Grant's entire body slumped. "Come on, Ethan—"

He turned his chair to face the window, knowing it was immature, childish, whatever, but he couldn't have this conversation right now. "I'll talk to you later."

Grant didn't move for what felt like a long time. Finally, he knocked twice on Ethan's desk, heaving a sigh, and then his footsteps retreated to the door. When it clicked behind him, Ethan fell forward, bracing his elbows on his knees and his face in his hands.

No way could he go in front of the camera again. It wasn't because of the scars, it was because of what the scars represented. There would be questions about why he'd stopped making videos, and he'd have to answer. He wasn't the charming, carefree Ethan Talley who could play video games like he didn't have any cares in the world. He didn't know how to smile like that anymore, how to exude that effortless confidence.

He wasn't that person.

And he didn't really want to be. Because that person killed his sister, broke up his family, and no longer had parents who spoke to him.

He dug the heel of his palms into his eyes and then leaned back in his chair, staring sightlessly out his windows, into the parking lot of the industrial park.

Of course, *he* knew why he'd been a little angry since Austin's wedding. He wasn't going to tell Grant that, because Grant was a gossiping old biddy. And as soon as Ethan confessed he couldn't get a woman out of his head, Grant would investigate like he was in the fucking CIA, and in a demented whisper-down-the-lane, Lissa would probably hear about it.

He swore he heard her laughter in his dreams. Or maybe his nightmares.

Her business card was burning a hole in his wallet. He should have thrown it away, but he couldn't bring himself to do it. And now it didn't matter because he had everything memorized anyway. He'd resisted calling and had even driven out of his way numerous times in the last couple of days so he didn't have to ride past her studio.

He turned back to his desk and tapped his fingers on the surface. A quick glance at his door verified his blinds were drawn and no one would see him inside having a silent freak-out.

That should have told him he would cave eventually.

He was self-aware enough to know that he was fucked up. And he was in no position to give anyone any part of himself. But Lissa hadn't asked for that. He'd asked for all he was willing to give, and she'd accepted with a smile.

And then offered him seconds.

He could take seconds. Double dip just once. She wasn't getting out of his head anytime soon, and if she was willing to help bank this fire in his belly that raged to touch her again, then why not? Why deny himself when he'd been doing it for all these years?

It didn't have to be a thing. They were consenting adults who liked sex. With each other.

It would help him forget about Grant's request and the fact that, yet again, his past was surging up to knock him on his ass. To Lissa, he was just Ethan Talley, some asshole magazine executive. Who could make her come twice.

He pulled his car keys out of the top drawer of his desk and jiggled them in his palm for a minute, frowning at them like they were a magic eight ball and would tell him his future.

Or what to do.

These feelings, this want, was all new to him. Or at least, new to the post-accident Ethan. He wasn't sure what to do with them, but the only thing that worked was when he was with her.

He fisted his keys and left his office.

Chapter Six

Daniel held up a pink boa and blew away a few stray feathers as they threatened to land on his head. "Well, that was fun."

Lissa plucked a riding crop off the satin-draped cushion. "It was, wasn't it?"

His cheeks were still pink, probably a flush left over from watching several lingerie-clad women spread out on set. "I really think we should offer a discount on boudoir shoots and do, like, one or two a day."

Lissa threw a set of furry handcuffs at him. "Oh, shut up."

"Hey, I spent a lot of time hunting down these props!"

Lissa laughed. "You did great, my young padawan. Now get going, I know you have a class soon."

He gazed around at the mess in their studio. "But—"

Lissa shook her head. "It's worse than it looks. Now shoo." With one last look, he scurried away. "Lock the door when you leave!" she called after him.

Ten minutes later, she was still cleaning up the props to the boudoir session she'd done that afternoon. A group of moms who'd all been friends in college decided they wanted to get the photos done together for their husbands and significant others. Lissa glanced over at the empty bottles of wine and grinned. It had been a blast.

There was a knock at the door, and Lissa glanced at the clock. They were closed, but sometimes people didn't see the sign, or it could be Daniel returning.

She wiped her hands and righted her clothes before walking to the front door. But when she pulled it open, instead of Daniel standing there, it was…Ethan.

Large aviator glasses covered his eyes, and again, he wore an all-black suit, this time with a dark blue patterned shirt underneath.

Her body heated immediately at the sight of him, easily recalling the sensation of being touched by those hands that now hung confidently at his sides. A large silver watch peeked out from the hem of his sleeve.

She'd thought about him every day—multiple times a day—since the wedding. She thought he'd never contact her again, but here he was, on the doorstep of her studio. She braced a hand above her head on the door. "You could have called, you know."

He jolted, and a furrow appeared between his brows, like he hadn't thought of that. "I didn't want to talk to you. I wanted to see you."

She snorted. "You're shit at seducing, you know that?"

His lips tilted down. "Do I need to seduce you?"

She cocked her head, eyeing the dark stubble on his jaw, those full lips. She huffed a laugh and shook her head then motioned for him to come into the studio. He stepped inside in two strides, and she shut the door behind him, locking it.

He watched her. "I can come back another time."

She waved a hand in dismissal. "It's fine. I'm just cleaning up from a shoot." She walked down the hallway into the studio, the click of his dress shoes following her.

Without pausing, she continued to clean, and after thirty seconds, he joined in silently, grabbing a trash bag in the corner to throw away the wine bottles and plastic cups. She wiped her hand on her forehead. "You don't have to do that."

He shot her a look like, *what else am I going to do?* and she ducked her head so he didn't see her smile. He looked ridiculous, dressed in a suit and picking up stray pink feathers to throw away.

He turned with his back to her, so she was able to study him uninterrupted. She wasn't sure what possessed her to leave him her card at the wedding, but she had. Now that he was here, even though she told herself not to get involved, that he was her golden ticket for her project, that didn't stop her body from coming alive at the sight of him.

She needed to send him on his way, or put the brakes on this. If she continued to sleep with him, it would fuck everything up. She'd have to tell him this couldn't happen again, that she didn't want it.

With a nod to herself, she turned around and continued to clean up. When a noise drew her attention, she looked over her shoulder to see Ethan wiping a table, a light purple feather boa wrapped around his neck. She began to laugh, and he stared at her with those ice-blue eyes. "What?"

"That just might be your color, Mr. Talley," she said, pointing to his feather scarf.

He seemed confused at first then glanced down at himself. He plucked at the boa. "Oh, uh, I just wrapped it around me to get it off the floor."

She pointed to a chest in the corner. "You can put it in there."

He made to walk to the chest but then stopped abruptly and glanced down at the table he'd been cleaning. With a raised eyebrow, he lifted a riding crop and a pair of handcuffs.

"Props," she explained.

"Props," he echoed.

"Yes."

"And exactly what kind of shoot were you doing, Miss Kingsman?"

The amusement in his voice surprised her. She turned around to face him and leaned against the wall behind her. "Boudoir."

He murmured an assent, his gaze on the end of the riding crop.

Something flashed over his eyes, and with a slight quirk to his lips, he stalked toward her. His expression held a predatory gleam, and while a huge part of her wanted to be his prey, the rational side told her to run.

Which she did. With a squeal, she launched herself away from him, but he was faster than her and had much longer legs. His arm wrapped around her waist, and then he hauled her back against his body. Her breath made an oomph sound and then she was laughing and squirming as he began to tickle her neck with the ends of the feather boa. "Stop, I'm ticklish!" She pushed on his arm, but it didn't budge. She managed to grab the riding crop out of his hand and reach around to give his thigh a firm hit.

He froze. And so did she.

His breath came fast against her ear. "Did you just… smack me?"

"Um…" she mumbled.

"You did, didn't you?" There was a smile in his voice. "You just smacked me with that crop."

"You were tickling me!" she yelled.

He loosened his arm, and she slipped away, dashing over to the chest and then pulling out a masquerade mask. It was green and black with feathers and sequins, and she held it up to her eyes with an attached stick. "Lissa's not here. Madam Bravo can answer any questions or concerns."

He laughed—a loud, raucous, deep-belly laugh. He looked as surprised as she was at the outburst of sound. Something deep inside of her unfurled at the sight of his beautiful face lit with humor. How had she ever thought his eyes were cold? They were anything but cold when he was like this.

He took a step toward her and she held an arm out to stop him, even though all she wanted to do was run into his arms and climb him.

"Madam Bravo," he said.

"Yes," she answered in a haughty voice.

"What kind of lingerie does Lissa have on?" He took several slow steps toward her. "I'm thinking something with satin and lace. Purple or pink." He was close now, so she had to lean her head back to look at him. She curled her hand behind her and rooted blindly in the box before her hand closed over exactly what she'd been looking for. Ethan's lips curled into a sensual smile. "I bet if I touch you, those panties will be soaked through, am I right?"

God, his voice. It did things to her, which was why she tossed out one last defense against Ethan Talley. From behind her back, she flung her arm above their heads. In the next second, glitter rained down.

She took that moment to get away, out from under Ethan's gaze, but once again, he was too fast for her. He gripped her wrist as he waved his hand and sputtered as the rainbow glitter coated them. "You think you're funny?" he asked, smirking.

As the glitter settled, she blinked away what had settled on her lashes. Ethan's hair was coated. He had a clump of gold glitter right on the edge of his nose and a couple on his lips. His dour jacket now looked…well, like he belonged in a Pride parade; glitter stuck to the fabric. She began to giggle, and laughter burst through his lips, despite his trying to contain it.

In the next instant, she was flat on her back on the floor,

right on that stupid fake white bearskin rug she'd bought as a prop. She wrapped her legs around Ethan's waist as his tongue slid into her mouth.

She thought about pushing him away, telling him she didn't want this, but that was a lie. Her hips were thrusting against the hardness in his groin, and her nipples were beaded and poking through her thin—pink satin and lace—bra.

Damn the man.

Whatever. One more time. This would be it, and then she had to find a way to ask him about the project. It wasn't her fault she was irresistible. And this was strictly about getting off. No emotions. It would be *fine.*

So she fumbled at his suit jacket, tugging it down his arms. With their lips still fused, he loosened his tie, and she bit and licked at the skin of his neck as he fumbled to undo his belt and zipper.

"I need inside you," he muttered. "Haven't thought of anything else for two fucking weeks but getting back inside you."

She pushed on his shoulders so he was forced to lean back. Then she gripped the hem of her short dress and tugged it up to over her head. Bracing her heels on the rug, she spread her legs. "Go on, get inside me then."

• • •

There was glitter everywhere. In her hair, shining off her dark skin, stuck in the fibers of this ugly bearskin rug.

She wore a pink satin and lace bra and matching thong. And she was spread out in front of him like a buffet of skin and glitter. He ran a finger down her throat, between her breasts, down to the waistband of her panties. A shudder wracked her body, but she stayed silent, biting her lip as he tugged her panties down her legs.

Her flesh was bare and glistening, and he did the exact thing he'd been dreaming about since the wedding. He lay down on his stomach, hooked her legs over his shoulders, and pressed his lips to her.

She squirmed under him and cried out as he licked and sucked at the sensitive flesh of her pussy. She wasn't silent or docile as he moved on to her clit. She rolled her hips and moaned, and he had to grip her hips hard to keep his mouth on her.

"Ethan." Her voice was breathless. "Don't stop, don't—" Her words cut out when he sucked on her clit. "Oh God, don't you fucking stop."

He let go of one of her thighs and slid a finger inside of her, plunging it in and out. The sounds around them were obscene, between the wet suction of his tongue on her flesh and the echo of her moans.

He blew on her clit, and she gasped. "You like my mouth on you?" He added another finger inside of her and crooked them.

She arched her back as he twisted his fingers and pumped them inside her. "Yes, I fucking love your mouth, now get back to work!"

He grinned and obliged, and it was only another couple of seconds before she shouted his name and came, her inner walls clamping down on his fingers like a vise.

He leaned back, shoving his pants down and reaching into his pocket for the condom he'd placed there with a wish.

He rolled it down his shaft as she watched, her eyes half-lidded. He tapped her sensitive skin with the head of his cock. "You ready?"

She reached for his cock and guided the tip inside of her as she licked her lips. "Fuck me."

With a snap of his hips, he buried himself to the root. "With pleasure."

He fell on top of her, with his forearms on either side of her head. He wasn't sure she'd want to kiss him. In his experience, not all women wanted to after he'd gone down on them, but she grabbed his face and tugged, smashing their lips together. In the next second, her tongue was in his mouth and he was fucking into her like his cock had a mind of its own.

Her nails scraped down his back, and he was strung so tight that a firm smack on his ass had him coming so hard his vision blurred.

With a moan, he managed to roll to the right and collapse at her side so his body didn't crush the woman beneath him. He peeked at her out of the corner of one eye. His arm was flung over her bare stomach and her hand was resting on the tops of her breasts, which rose and fell as she gulped air.

She rolled her head to the side and blinked at him, and then her lips stretched into a wide grin. She plucked something off the end of his nose, and he wiggled it before sneezing. She laughed and held up a chunk of glitter that must have been stuck to his face.

"Did I...?" he cleared his throat. "Um... Did I fuck you with glitter on my nose?"

She nodded, her eyes shining, her lips twitching like she couldn't contain her glee.

"I trust you not to tell anyone about this," he said as he sat up.

Her face fell and he loomed over her to say gravely, "Glitter sex would ruin my brooding rep, wouldn't you say?"

She laughed, curling onto her side as he stood up and tucked himself back into his clothes. With a hand arched over her head, she played with the ends of her curls as she watched him get redressed.

He glanced around her studio. "This is, uh, a nice place."

"Thanks." She stood up and pulled her dress on over her head.

His back itched, and he reached around, finding a small patch of glitter stuck to his spine. He sighed. "I'll still be finding this stuff on me a year from now, won't I?"

She walked up to him and smoothed his tie. "Yep. Sorry about that."

"You sound anything but sorry."

"I'm not sorry at all."

She turned away with a smirk over her shoulder and continued to clean up. He didn't help this time. He would in a minute, but first he wanted a chance to admire her as she moved about the room.

She was perfection, and she smelled like it, too. Years ago, before the accident, he would have asked her out, he would have showered her with gifts and maybe even asked her to be his.

But now, all he had to give were orgasms. Thank God he was still able to do that. Although he couldn't understand why she was putting up with this. Didn't she want someone who could give her more?

"What are you getting out of this?" he asked.

She froze and turned slowly on her heel, head cocked. "Excuse me?"

He licked his lips and worked out the words in his head before he spoke. "You're...you. You look like that, and you're funny and charming and..." He waved his hand to the pictures on the wall. "You're clearly talented, too. So why are you okay with what we're doing?"

She frowned at that and then turned fully with her hand on her hip. "Why are *you* okay with it?"

"Because...I get to have sex with you."

Her top teeth poked out to nibble on her bottom lip. "Okay, well I get to have sex with you. Why do I have to have another reason?"

She wasn't cooperating, and this was frustrating him. Was

she hiding something? "Because you have to!"

Her eyebrows flew up. "What?"

"Look, even if you did just want sex, you can't possibly be content with me when there are dozens of other men with fewer…issues."

"Even if?" she countered. "Do you ever listen to a word that comes out of my mouth? You're always searching for ulterior motives and there are none. I want to have sex with you. I don't want a relationship right now. I'm busy with my job, and since you're on the same page, it's a win-win. Why do you have to look deeper?"

He ran a hand through his hair and turned away, trying to sort out why exactly he was bothered by this. But his thoughts were a jumble, especially because his brain was orgasm-addled. He shook his head. "Okay."

She stepped toward him. "Okay what?"

"Okay, you're right. I don't know what got into me."

"Look, Ethan—"

He tugged her to him with a yank on her wrist, and she smashed into his chest. With her wrist clasped behind her back, he pressed a quick kiss to her lips. When he leaned back, her eyes were closed, and he spotted some glitter left over on her eyelids. Before he did something crazy—like kiss her eyelids, or wipe away the glitter, or anything else that could be misconstrued as something more affectionate—he released her and stepped back.

Her eyes popped open, and she must have sensed the change in his behavior, because she swallowed and nodded, a strained smile on her lips.

This would have to be it. He was getting too caught up in her, too worried about her feelings and his feelings and if they meshed and…he couldn't do this. The complications and everything that went along with giving someone else a piece of him.

He stepped back, and her body drifted forward, as if she planned to follow, but her feet stayed in place. He shoved his hands in his pockets and looked everywhere but at her. "Do you need me to stay and clean up? Or…"

They both knew that was an empty question. He was planning to leave.

She shook her head. "It's fine. I'll handle it."

He glanced around the studio, at the floor and walls and all the places that weren't the glitter-covered Lissa in front of him. He cleared his throat. "Right. So, uh, thanks for letting me in."

"Thanks for stopping by," she said.

Fucking awkward. This was it. He was done after this. He might not show his face at his office for a week. Finally, he met her warm brown gaze. "You take care, Lissa."

She opened her mouth, as if to say something, but then she shut her lips with a shake of her head. When she opened her mouth again, all she said was, "You, too, Ethan. You, too."

And then he was out the door, wondering how long he could deal with this glitter on his skin, because he wasn't sure he wanted to wash off the last scent of Lissa any time soon.

Chapter Seven

She'd chickened out.

She could have asked him right then. Right there. But his posture had screamed, "Back off," his expression more vulnerable than she'd seen him before. So she'd kept her mouth shut out of fear of offending him or hurting him or…

Fuck.

She told herself it had nothing to do with the fact that they'd slept together. Twice. She cared about him as much as anyone else off the street. He wasn't different. He wasn't special.

She gripped the broom tighter as she swept up the piles of glitter off the floor. That hadn't been the smartest idea she'd ever had, but it'd sure been fun. Biting her lip, she glanced at the bearskin rug. That was…going to need to be cleaned.

She laughed to herself and continued to sweep. When her studio was in some sort of order again, she sat down at her desk so she could determine whether she had enough energy to cook dinner at home or call out. She shared her apartment with her brother, and while it was nice to have help on rent, it wasn't so nice to be home when he was experimenting with different foods or when he had girls over.

Especially when he had girls over.

She blew out a breath and was about to pick up the phone to order a pizza when there was a knock at the door.

She froze, as if the person knocking could see her, even though the door wasn't even visible from where she sat. If it was Ethan again…well, she didn't have the energy to deal with him right now.

Her phone chimed and she glanced at it, then smiled.

Come get your door before I eat all this sushi myself

Her brother could be so thoughtful sometimes. Although, thank God he hadn't come about a half hour earlier. She'd already slipped off her shoes, so she trotted to the door in her bare feet and flung open the door. Angel brushed past her, two large paper bags in his hands. He shot her a grin—Rona's grin—and Lissa's heart clenched, like it always did.

"Hey, L." He leaned in and brushed his lips across her forehead. "Hungry?"

"How'd you know?" She followed him as he walked down her hallway and dropped the bags on a table beside her desk. He pulled up a chair, and she sank down in hers. His hands were in the open bags before she could blink. "You hungry, too?"

"Starved." He handed her some California rolls while he dug into his spicy eel ones. "Work was insane today. I'm exhausted."

"Busy?"

He stuck a roll in his mouth and talked around it. "Full moon or something? People were nuts." He leaned back in his chair and glanced at her studio behind them then jerked a thumb at the bearskin rug still on the floor. "You shooting porn in here now? Told you I could hire you at Foot Locker if you need money."

She laughed and shoved his shoulder. "Shut up, I was doing boudoir shoots." *And a non-filmed porno.*

He raised an eyebrow. "Oh yeah? Any honeys?"

"All the honeys had significant others."

"Damn," he muttered. Angel was always *between* girls since he changed them out so often. Little less often than his shoes.

"Hey," she said, swirling her roll in soy sauce so she didn't have to look Angel in the eye. Now that there'd been another *incident*, she couldn't keep her discovery to herself anymore. "You remember E-Rad?"

Angel didn't say anything for a minute, and his chair squeaked. "E-Rad! Oh yeah, the video game dude. Man, he was the shit. Haven't thought about him for years. He disappeared. What, they find his body in a river somewhere?"

Oh, she'd found his body all right, alive and well. She glanced up at her brother. "So I'm going to tell you something, but you can't tell anyone, okay?"

His eyes widened. "Did you kill E-Rad?"

"Will you shut up? No one killed him, you doofus."

He grinned. "I know, I was just kidding you."

"I'm serious, though. Look at me. You can't tell anyone what I'm going to tell you."

Angel nodded soberly. "Okay, okay."

She blew out a breath. She needed to tell someone, and she trusted her brother more than anyone in the world. "I think I met him. Or, I know I met him, I mean, I'm almost positive the guy I met is him."

Angel pushed his container of sushi aside and leaned forward on her desk, hands clasped together. She had his full attention now. "Start from the beginning."

So she did, from meeting him at *Gamers* to his scars. She didn't mention that they'd now had sex twice, because her brother really didn't need to know that. "I'd recognize that voice anywhere. But he's definitely not the same person."

"It's been, what? Close to ten years? Of course he isn't the same person."

"Yeah, I know that. This doesn't seem like regular growing pains, though. And clearly something happened to give him those scars."

Angel chewed his lip. "Damn, that guy was the shit. Can't believe you found him."

"Yeah, but he doesn't know I know who he is. And… something tells me he left that life behind."

"But he owns a gaming magazine now."

"I saw the interview. Nowhere is he mentioned as being the former E-Rad. Wouldn't that be something you'd tell a reporter?"

Angel nodded thoughtfully. "Hm, yeah, I guess so."

Lissa chewed her last roll and swallowed. There were so many questions, and while she wanted answers, part of her wasn't sure she was ready for the truth. There were so many secrets, so many dark shadows in Ethan's eyes and…maybe they were better left there.

"You're thinking of asking him to be in your project, aren't you?" Angel asked.

She sighed. "I was…or, I still am, I guess. I don't know. I think he'd be a great draw but…" She'd screwed him. Twice. And couldn't seem to help herself whenever he was around.

"Why are your cheeks red?" Angel demanded.

She jerked her head up. "What?"

He pointed at her face. "There was a definite flush there."

She fidgeted her hands in her lap and gritted her teeth. "You're making stuff up."

"Do you have a crush on this guy? You're making that face you always do before you nudge me and tell me some dude's hot."

"I am not," she huffed.

"You are too."

"Fine! Yes, he's hot, now drop it."

Angel didn't look like he wanted to drop it, but she glared at him until he sighed and ate the rest of his sushi.

After cleaning up dinner, Angel headed out while Lissa shut down the studio for the night. She took one more glance at the photo of Ethan in her secret folder. "What are your secrets, baby?" she whispered to herself.

If the look on Ethan's face when he left earlier was any indication, it was going to be an uphill battle to get him to talk to her again. She told herself this was all for Rona, but part of her knew this craving for his company had nothing to do with her project. And everything to do with how he made her feel.

• • •

Chloe sat cross-legged on his floor while he stretched out on the couch behind her. She cursed as the lizard-like creature she was directing on the TV screen fell down a hole.

Ethan snorted and pulled her out with his lizard tail.

"Tails are so handy," she said. "I want a tail in real life."

"Evolution had other ideas," he muttered.

Chloe had brought him soup for dinner. Even though he was perfectly capable of feeding himself, Chloe's soup was incredible and he would never turn it down. And then, like always, she stayed to play video games.

This game was called *Lizard Master*, and it was a PG-13 game that *Gamers* had been sent to review. Ethan rather liked it. It was no *Aric's Revenge*, but there was a lot to do and it was completely appropriate for preteens. "You want to give this to Sydney to try?" he asked.

Chloe's head nodded from her seat on the floor. "Sure."

"Graphics are good. I could probably count the scales

on my guy's back—Oh!" He winced as the tip of his tail was severed by an enemy's sword. "Shit! Oh well, that's not going to leave a mark because…" He paused as his tail regenerated, and he grinned. "Ta-da! I'm basically a fucking starfish. You can't kill me by severing limbs!" He snorted. "Amateur."

He stopped when he realized Chloe wasn't playing anymore. She had twisted at the waist and was watching him with an amused glint in her eyes.

"What's that look for?"

"Because you can take the E-Rad out from in front of the camera, but you can't keep the vocal gamer out of E-Rad."

He didn't like where this was going, and his palms began to sweat. "I was just making conversation."

"No, you weren't. You were commentating as if I wasn't even here. If I closed my eyes, it would be like it was—" She stopped talking when he abruptly shut down everything with one click from his master control. Chloe's face dropped. "Ethan—"

He met her gaze, and he knew his expression was blank, because if he dropped an ounce of control, he'd sneer at her. And his sister didn't deserve that. So with every muscle tight in order to focus on neutrality, he said, "As soon as you open your eyes, you'll see nothing is like it was. Nothing."

He stood up, hating to see the devastated look on his sister's face, but not wanting to talk about this. He made his way to the kitchen and pulled a beer out of the fridge. "Want one?" He held one out to Chloe, who had followed him into the kitchen.

She shook her head. "My eyes are open, Ethan. You're the one who refuses to see anything but your own misery."

He whirled to face her. "Why am I not allowed to be like this? Can't I handle everything the way I want to? On my own terms?"

She pursed her lips and dropped her eyes, shuffling her

feet in her leopard print flats. "I'm sorry I brought it up, but I worry about you."

"You don't need to worry."

She glanced up and braced herself on the counter. "You can't just say that and expect me to go, 'oh, okay, well then, everything's peachy.' Not while you hole yourself up in this house, work your ass off, and don't date."

"I don't need a wife to be happy."

She threw up her hands. "I never said you did. But you used to love to socialize. You loved women and dating and…" She let her voice trail off then bit her lip. "You used to love it all. And now, I'm not sure what you love anymore."

Her words were slicing and dicing, when he hadn't thought there was much left to hurt. He gulped his beer. After he swallowed, he said. "I love *you*."

She took a step closer. "I know you do. It's who you *don't* love that worries me." He didn't meet her eyes, choosing to focus on peeling the label off his beer bottle. She sighed. "You don't love yourself, and there's nothing I can do to change that."

He didn't know what to say to that, because they both knew she was right. There was no point in confirming.

When he didn't respond, she grabbed her purse. "I have to go."

He nodded.

She stood in front of him until he finally looked up. Her cheeks were flushed and her eyes a little wet. She smiled sadly. "I love you, and I think I'm a pretty good judge of character, don't you think?"

When the only answer was his silence, she squeezed his arm and left.

He stood there for a long moment, until the rest of his beer was lukewarm and he had to pour it down the drain. He had a lot of issues, but drinking too heavily was not one of them, thank God.

Chloe had been right—he used to love to date. He loved women and they loved him. Before the accident, he'd managed to stay friends with a lot of his exes too. After the accident...well, he stopped returning their calls and emails until they moved on with their lives.

He was so out of practice that this thing with Lissa was throwing him off balance. *This thing.* Yeah, he didn't know how else to describe it, because he didn't know what it was. It'd been two weeks since he'd visited her at her studio, and the distance had done nothing to curb his interest in her.

His body heated when he remembered the tickle of the glitter and the soft brush of that bearskin rug on his skin. Her fingers and her lips and her soft moans.

That mouth.

And that fucking glitter, which he was still finding in odd places on his body at odd times. Just the other day, he'd been in his office and a piece fell out of his hair. He'd showered many times since the afternoon in her studio. That fucking glitter was like herpes.

He shook his head and glanced at the dark TV. It'd been a long time since he'd thought about E-Rad. Today's streaming services had changed the game of video game commentating a little bit, but at the time, he'd been king of the YouTube gaming community. Software companies sent him games by the truckloads. He had advertisers paying top dollar for a thirty second spot on his videos.

All he had to do was videotape himself playing video games and...talk. He'd been good at talking once. Charming, even. He snorted to himself. That was another life. Chloe didn't know what she was talking about. He didn't have it in him anymore. Hell, he barely remembered what he'd done. It'd been so long since he'd seen one of his videos. Because of the speed at which the community moved, he was forgotten.

And he liked it that way. No questions. He was only Ethan Talley, co-owner of *Gamers* magazine and local shut-in.

His iPad sat on the counter, and with one finger, he slid it over in front of him. His videos were still there. He didn't bother taking them down when he still got advertising money from them. Nothing huge, because he wasn't a household name anymore.

He pulled up his channel. His most popular videos were for *World of Warcraft*. His finger hovered over the play button for a video as he stared into the small thumbnail of his face in the lower left corner. In the screenshot, he was smiling, all white teeth and blue eyes and dark hair. He had stubble, but that didn't hide the fact that his face was unblemished.

That was back when he hadn't known how much he could fuck up.

That kid had no fucking clue.

With a stab, Ethan closed out the browser and shoved the iPad away. It nearly went skittering off the counter, and he had to catch it before it fell. Placing it down gently with a calmness he didn't feel, he walked away.

He couldn't stand to look at that guy. He hated that guy.

Pacing in his living room, he ran his hands through his hair. His nerves were shot after the conversation with Chloe and the close call of watching his old videos.

He needed something to calm him, to make him forget. To make him fucking happy for once. And all he could think about was Lissa.

Her laughter and the smell of her skin, and that silky voice. He'd been trying to stay away from her, worried they'd both get too involved, but fuck it. He wanted her.

He stared at his cell phone on the coffee table, just sitting there, daring him to pick it up.

He could call, just to feel her out. Maybe after he'd left so oddly from her studio, she'd be cold. Or maybe she'd be happy.

The sex had been amazing. She'd be happy. Right?

He snatched the phone up and dialed the number he had memorized from her business card before he chickened out. Sweat beaded on his temple and he ran his hands through his hair, gripping the strands and squeezing until the pain in his scalp centered him.

One ring.

Two rings.

Then the click of someone picking up. Ethan sucked in a breath and held it.

"Memories by Lissa, how may I help you?"

The voice was decidedly male and decidedly not Lissa. All the bravado Ethan had managed to cobble together fled like leaves scattered in the wind. He exhaled sharply. "Um, yes, I'm just wondering your hours."

There was a hesitation. "We'll, we're open until five, but we work by appointment only." Of course, Jesus, this wasn't Target. He floundered, but before he could speak again, the man on the other end of the line beat him to it. "Would you like to make an appointment? Are you interested in Lissa's services?"

Hell yeah, he was interested in Lissa's services, but he didn't think this man—probably her assistant—wanted to know exactly which services he wanted. Because they didn't involve a camera.

He cleared his throat. "Is Lissa available today?"

"No, I'm sorry, she's doing some family portraits over at Willow Park."

Ethan didn't know what else to say. "Right, er, thank you. Let me check my schedule and call back." He ended the call as the man was in mid-sentence.

He let his head fall onto his fireplace mantel, where he banged it a couple of times, then he lifted it and rubbed the abused skin on his forehead.

At this moment, he wished he had a dog. A dog that needed a walk. A dog that needed a walk at Willow Park and just happened to leap to the attention of a certain photographer with a great laugh and perfect ass.

Ethan loved his imaginary dog already.

He rubbed his chin. He didn't have to have a dog to go to the park. He could just…go. And walk, or do whatever it was people did at parks. And if he happened to see Lissa, then that was just a bonus.

He grabbed his jacket and was out the door before he lost this resurgence of courage.

Chapter Eight

Lissa smiled at her client and ruffled the hair of the boy at her side. "You want to try one more shot? The little bridge over there makes a really cool photograph, especially with the colored leaves behind it."

Amanda, her client, perked up. "That would be great!" She looked down at her son. "Can we do one more, buddy?"

The six-year-old had been a trooper and even though his shoulders sagged, he nodded. The park was nearly empty this afternoon, so Lissa had been able to work with Amanda and her son, with minimal distractions. Lissa enjoyed the work, and capturing this moment in time for families meant a lot to her. She wished she had more pictures of her and Rona.

They'd been blessed with an overcast sky for most of the day, which was perfect for portraits, but by the time they made it over to the bridge, the sun had emerged, bringing its crappy light with it. Lissa grabbed her sun shade out of her bag and bit her lip as she thought about where to place it to best shield her clients. She preferred to control the light, and the sun didn't work well with that plan. Also? There was no one to hold the shade. Usually that job was handled by Daniel, but he'd had another appointment back at the studio.

She heard the beep of a car locking and turned around, spotting a black SUV but no person in sight. Something about the SUV was familiar, but she couldn't place it.

"Lissa?" Amanda asked. "Everything okay?"

She focused back on her client. "Yeah, I'm going to need to shade you from the sun, but my assistant isn't here to hold the shade."

Michael peered over her shoulder. "Can we ask that man?"

Lissa turned around to see Ethan Talley leaning against his SUV, arms crossed, sunglasses hiding his eyes. *What is he doing here?* Her curiosity didn't stop her from noting that he looked imposing. And fucking hot.

Lissa turned back around, hoping her face wasn't turning red. "Um…"

"That man is dressed nicely," Amanda said. "We probably shouldn't bother him—"

"Mister!" Michael called, waving his hands. "Could you help us?"

Lissa closed her eyes briefly, muttering under her breath, hoping Ethan said he was busy, that he had to get back to work, but, try as she might, she couldn't drown out the sound of his footsteps swishing through the grass as he made his way toward them.

When he sounded close, she plastered a smile on her face and turned to him. "Hi."

She couldn't see his eyes, and maybe that was a good thing, because he stared a moment longer than was acceptable. She swore she could feel the heat of his gaze burning through those sunglasses. "Hello," he finally said. "How can I help?"

God, this was embarrassing. Stupid goddamn sun. She cleared her throat and held out the shade, extending the pole attached so he could hold it out over the clients. "I need you to hold this. Please."

He took it from her, and she opened her mouth to direct him where to stand, then figured that was a waste. Easier to show him.

She gripped his biceps, the expensive fabric of his jacket soft on her palms, and moved his body where she wanted it, positioning his arms so they were in the right place. He accepted all this with a small smile of amusement. Right as she was about to walk away, he muttered, "I could get used to you manhandling me."

She shot him a glare. "I already have an assistant."

His lips quirked up. "Right, but I'd do it for free. Or at least, you wouldn't have to pay me in money." He waggled his eyebrows and it was so ridiculous and corny and out of character for the stone-faced Ethan Talley that she laughed. Loudly.

"Do you two know each other?" Amanda asked.

Lissa cleared her throat, ignoring the smug look on Ethan's face. "Um, we've met briefly. Through friends."

Amanda turned to Ethan. "Well, nice to meet you. And thanks for your help."

"Anytime," Ethan said.

Lissa sighed and worked on ignoring Ethan's presence and getting her shots. Michael had been patient for a long time, but it was clear now that he was tired and cranky. He was making faces and slumping, and Lissa feared all of these bridge photos would be a waste. She did notice that the boy kept sneaking glances at Ethan. And he must have noticed, too. He took off his sunglasses and slipped them into his pocket. "I know pictures aren't fun, but this is a nice thing you're doing for your mom."

Michael straightened his shoulder slightly. "Yeah?"

Ethan nodded. "Of course. It says something about you as

a young man that you're doing something nice for the woman who is raising you."

Michael's shoulders went even straighter, and he visibly gathered himself—all four feet of him—and smiled the brightest smile Lissa had seen yet.

She shot Ethan a smile, and he nodded in her direction, his lips curving, and that did something weird and warm and liquefying to her belly.

Once she was satisfied with her shots, she directed Ethan to drop the shade, which he did with a roll of his shoulder. He walked up to Michael and shook his hand, like they were equals, and the little boy looked up in awe.

She walked up and stood next to Ethan. "You did great."

Michael ducked his head and shuffled his feet, peeking at both of them out of the corner of his eye.

Lissa stepped forward and shook Amanda's hand, ever aware of Ethan's presence at her back. "I'll have these edited and proofs sent to you in two weeks."

"That's great, Lissa. You were wonderful to work with. You came highly recommended, and I see why."

Lissa stuffed down the burst of pride. "Well, you haven't seen the photos yet, they could be really horrible and blurry."

Amanda laughed. "I don't think they will be."

Lissa shook her head. "No, I don't think so, either."

She held out her hand for Michael to high-five, which he slapped with a burst of energy. Amanda patted his back and directed him to her car. "I need to get him home. Thanks again!"

"Anytime."

Lissa watched as they walked away. Then she slowly turned to face Ethan, who pierced her with those light blue eyes of his. She motioned to his shoulder. "Is it sore from holding the shade?"

He scoffed. "No."

"You did a great job with that little boy."

A shimmer of unease over the compliment flitted across his features. "I could tell he was kind of over it for the day. But where you had them standing was beautiful, so it seemed important those pictures come out well."

She cocked her head, studying him, and his gaze shifted away. That meant something to her, that he'd cared about her job and those family pictures. Especially when he'd been so anti-pictures himself. "Does that mean you see value in photographs?"

His expression hardened a minute, and although he seemed about to snap out a retort, he hesitated. When he spoke, his voice was soft. "I see the value. I just don't see the value in photographs of myself."

She took a chance. "What about if your mom asked?"

She was on thin ice, his sharp blue gaze told her that much, as well as his flinch and the words spoken through gritted teeth. "She knows better than to ask."

Lissa filed that away and decided to change the subject before she angered Ethan further. Also, he'd done her a favor, so what kind of asshole was she if she repaid him by prodding at his soft spots?

She tilted her head and smiled. "So, Daniel's going to be disappointed when I tell him he's fired."

Ethan's expression softened when he realized she wasn't going to keep up with her line of questioning. "I'm sure Grant can manage the magazine on his own, so I can pursue my career in sun shading."

She laughed and began to put her camera and supplies away. When she was finished, she stood up and tugged the strap of her bag over her shoulder. "So are you going to tell me it's coincidence you're here?"

He shook his head. "Nope, I called, and your newly-fired assistant said you'd be here."

She wasn't sure how to answer that, so she started to walk toward the parking lot. Ethan fell in step beside her. After the wedding, she'd given up hope he'd call, and she'd been trying to find a way to contact him about her project. At least, that was what she told herself, not that she craved to feel his hands on her body again.

She nodded. "Okay, and so why are *you* here?"

His answer came quick. "Because this is where you are."

Heat pooled in her belly as they reached his SUV. She stopped as he leaned against it, watching her. "And why do you want to be where I am, Ethan?"

He looked away, his jaw shifting. She watched his profile, waiting with rising anxiety on his answer. Finally he turned to her, and those ice-blue eyes froze her in place. "I want you."

He wasn't within touching distance and yet she could still feel the heat of his fingers on her skin, the sound of his voice in her ear, the fullness of his cock filling her. She shifted her weight from foot to foot. She hadn't expected that, and even though her brain was screaming at her to knock this off, to cool down and focus on what she wanted from him, her body was demanding attention first, and it wanted him in a totally different way. "I want you, too."

His hand shot out and gripped her wrist. In the next second, she was pressed against the side of his car, his big body blocking hers, preventing her from moving. Which was fine, because she didn't want to move. He placed her camera on the hood of his car, slid his hand around her neck, and then kissed her.

She opened for him immediately, gripping his biceps and digging her fingernails into the thick material of his jacket.

His thigh nudged between her legs and rubbed against her. She rutted against his leg, unable to help herself, because after the pent-up frustration of the last couple of days, she was ready to combust.

She pulled away from the kiss and laid her forehead on his shoulder. She was thrusting against him, and in the back of her mind, she wondered what the hell she was doing at twenty-fucking-nine years old, dry-humping this cold bastard in a public park, but their cars were the only two in the lot.

No one was around and she was so desperate to come, she didn't care.

He gripped the back of her neck, keeping her pressed to him, and nudged his thigh closer, changing the angle so she was hitting just the right spot every time she rolled her hips into him.

"Oh God," she muttered. "Did you plan this? Wanting to make me so fucking horny I'd come like a teenage girl in the back of a limo after prom?"

He laughed softly, his voice husky. "It's taking every effort not to push you to your knees. Does that sound like your prom? That doesn't sound like mine."

She couldn't even laugh, because now she was salivating over sucking him off. She shoved her face into his neck, rooting until her lips found skin under his collar. "You want that?" she muttered against him as she chased her orgasm. "My slutty mouth around your dick?"

He was thrusting against her, too, his breathing ragged. "You come and we'll see if we can put those lips to work, punish you for teasing me."

"Yes," she moaned.

He spoke in her ear, his words a harsh whisper. "I'll keep you there, on your knees, my cock in your mouth until you swallow me. All of me. Would like you that, Lissa?"

Her face heated, her spine tingled. She was right there, just another push…

"That red lipstick would look great on my cock, you think?"

That was it. That was all she needed, thinking about

leaving her mark behind on his skin. She came with a cry as she thrust against his thigh, the hard metal of his car at her back.

She was still trembling when he pulled open the back door and guided her inside with a firm hand on her arm. He sat on the black leather and looked her in the eye. "On your knees."

She sank down somewhat gracelessly because her legs were jelly. Cocking an eyebrow, she said, "I didn't hear a please."

He clenched his jaw, but his lips twitched. "Please."

She reached for his fly. "I always reward good manners."

Chapter Nine

This was not going according to plan.

By the time Ethan had parked, he'd told himself he wouldn't jump on her like a sex-starved heathen. He hadn't even planned to talk to her. He only wanted to observe her as she worked. But as soon as she'd needed his help and he'd been in her presence again, he no longer had control over himself.

All he knew was that he needed her again.

So as her hands deftly undid the button on his pants and slid down his fly, he decided this was an excellent plan. Yep. This one. He was very, very thankful for the darkly tinted windows in his vehicle.

She pulled his hard cock out through the opening and stroked it a few times with a murmur of appreciation. Then she stuck out that pink tongue and, with a glance up with those big brown eyes, she licked the tip.

He sucked in a breath and squirmed. He remembered she rewarded manners, so as she took her time lapping around the head of his dick, he didn't urge her to get on with it. As much as he wanted to come, he also wanted to draw this out. The sight of Lissa on her knees, all that beautiful hair in between his thighs, well, he didn't want this over any time soon.

Nimble fingers slid along the base of his cock and then dipped lower to his balls. He shifted in the seat so she had better access, and she pulled off to grin up at him. "I love your taste."

He swallowed. "I love watching you taste me."

Another twitch of those lips and then she swallowed him to the root.

He fisted his hands and somehow managed to keep himself from crying out like a...well, like a teenage virgin at prom. Lissa knew how to handle a cock, how to roll his balls in her hand and swirl her tongue under the head.

He reached a hand out and she pulled off for a minute to say, "Touch anything but the hair." Then she was back, taking him into her mouth.

His hand hovered mid-air before it descended onto her shoulder. He squeezed then trailed his fingers up her neck until he gently held her chin.

She moaned and her eyes drifted shut.

He didn't guide her—she didn't need it—but it turned him on to see his hand there. Her fingers dug into his thighs, and he leaned his head back on the seat, telling himself not to delay this, but to enjoy it. Lissa didn't seem in a hurry, either.

But it wouldn't last; it couldn't, especially not with her skilled tongue, her soft moans. He gazed down at her and brushed her hollowed cheeks with his fingers. "This mouth." He wiped away some moisture that had leaked out of her eye. "I like everything you do with this mouth."

She shifted beneath him, her eyelashes fluttering.

"You love this, don't you?" he asked softly.

Despite her bobbing head, her nod was unmistakable. She renewed her efforts, twisting her hand at the base, and when she tilted her mouth at the head to shoot him a sultry look, that was all it took. He gripped her shoulder and came with a soft groan, pulsing into her mouth while she kept up the tight suction.

He let his head fall back again, this time unable to lift it again. He felt her tuck his softened cock back into his pants. Then her scent was all around him again as she settled herself astride his lap. His arms automatically wrapped around her back while she loomed over him, all smeared lipstick and self-satisfied smile.

She nibbled on his lips, slightly tentative, as if she wasn't sure he'd want to kiss her. But fuck that, he did want to kiss her, so he pressed her close and opened his mouth to delve his tongue inside. She sighed and relaxed in his arms, spearing her fingers through his hair as she gripped his head.

The kiss was slow and lazy and not urgent, just a gentle meshing of tongues. When she pulled back, she ran a finger down the side of his face. She lingered on his jaw, her gaze following her hand, and it took a minute in his post-orgasmic bliss to notice she was looking at his scars.

No. It might be backward, but his dick in her mouth didn't afford her *him*. Even though he registered this was going to crash and burn, he couldn't stop his knee-jerk reaction.

He stiffened, immediately on guard, and his head shot up so fast they nearly collided noses. She reared back, her hands dropping to his shoulders. "I—"

But he couldn't look her in the eye anymore, because he'd see pity there. Sympathy. He'd see himself reflected in those brown eyes, and he wouldn't like what he saw. He gently guided her off him, and she stared at him while he fumbled to open up the door. He stepped out, righting his clothes as well as he could and glancing around the parking lot.

There were a couple of cars at the opposite end now, but Ethan didn't see any people. He turned around as Lissa exited the vehicle, and he cleared his throat. "Thank you—"

She held up a hand, and her eyes flashed. "Do not *thank me* for that. Please."

He clenched his jaw and gave her a stiff nod. She stood with her hands on his hips, studying his face, but he carefully kept his gaze trained over her shoulder.

"So that's how it's going to be, huh?" she asked.

"I don't know what that means." His voice was stiff and so cold it even made him shiver.

She sighed and moved to take her camera bag off his car. She checked the contents, muttering to herself about how stupid she'd been to leave it out where anything could have been taken.

"If anything was stolen, I'd have paid for—"

"Oh my God, Ethan, shut the fuck up. I wouldn't let you pay me for anything that was stolen, because it happened while I was giving you a blow job. I don't want your money or your thanks. I'd like you to look me in the eye and quit treating me like what we did was wrong or that you took advantage of me."

He took a deep breath and steeled himself with a neutral expression before meeting her gaze.

She searched his face, and after a minute, her lips thinned and she nodded. "Right, okay then. I don't know what...I don't know what's going on to make you turn into stone like I'm fucking Medusa, but you know the best thing about hookups, Ethan? The best thing about not getting emotionally attached?"

He didn't answer.

She hiked her bag over her shoulder and shot him a withering look. "The best thing is that I don't care."

And then she walked away to a green Jeep in the corner of the lot. He stayed where he was, staring off into the park while he heard her start up her vehicle and drive away in a squeal of tires.

I don't care.

Yeah, well he didn't, either.

...

By the time Lissa parked outside her apartment, her hands had stopped shaking. She'd gone from mild annoyance to anger about what happened back there. Against Ethan's car. Inside it. Then outside it again.

"I don't care. I don't care," she chanted to herself. But that anger was slowly shifting to concern the more she replayed everything in her head.

At first she'd felt casted aside, but now that she thought more about it, everything about Ethan's posture and expression afterward had been about him. She might have done or said something to prompt him to retreat into himself, but it was his choice to act like that. It wasn't about her, so she shouldn't have cared, but yet she did. This man clearly wanted her, enough to follow her to the park while she was working.

Why was he such a hard bastard to read? And what was he hiding behind that impassive expression and scarred skin?

It wasn't about the project anymore. Well, it was, but it was also about him. She hadn't been there for her sister, and Rona wasn't alive anymore. She wasn't substituting Ethan for Rona, but she couldn't get him out of her head. What if she could help him? He was in her head now, on her skin. When he let his guard drop down, when he allowed himself to laugh in her studio, it had been a wonderful thing. She'd seen glimpses of the old charming E-Rad shine through. But his laugh had been rusty. He was exactly the type of person she was trying to reach with her project.

She didn't know what do anymore, but she couldn't forget about Ethan, no matter how much she wanted to.

After trudging up the stairs with her camera bag, she opened her door to the sound of a pounding base and the smell of something burning. She groaned to herself as Angel let loose a loud rap verse.

She dropped her bags and walked over to the TV, where the music was coming from, and immediately muted it.

Angel cursed and spun around, a towel thrown over his shoulder, eyes wide. "Hey! I didn't hear you."

She raised her eyebrows. "Yeah, I gathered that, seeing as I couldn't hear myself think with how loud your music was."

"Sorry, when you're not here, I let loose."

She snorted and flopped down on the couch. Their apartment was an open floor plan, so she could see him working away in the kitchen from the living room. "Whatcha' burning?"

"I'm not burning anything!" he protested.

"It smells—"

"That was so ten minutes ago," he said. "Everything's fine now."

She made a note to check the trash for whatever he'd burned. Hopefully it wasn't still sizzling. "Okay, so what are you cooking?"

"Uh, some sausage thing."

That was specific. "Am I going to like this sausage thing?"

"Sure."

That didn't sound promising. But she didn't really care. She slipped off her shoes and tucked her feet under her, then lay on her side with her head on a pillow.

She hadn't realized she'd drifted off until something shook her shoulder.

"Lissa?" her brother said softly.

She blinked her eyes open to see him standing above her, holding a bowl of soup and frowning. She stretched with her arms over her head and sat up. "Wow, sorry about that."

"You never fall asleep like that," he said, still frowning.

She shrugged, not wanting to tell her an afternoon delight made her crave nap time. "I don't know, just tired I guess."

He didn't seem appeased. "You need to work less."

"Quit mothering me. Now, are you going to give me that bowl or just tempt me with the delicious smells?"

Now he grinned. "It's a sausage chili."

She took the bowl from him, wrapping her hands around the warm ceramic. "Mmm." She took a bite and let the bold flavors rest on her tongue. "This is incredible, Angel."

He stood in front of her, wringing his hands, waiting for her reaction. "Yeah?"

"Of course."

He fist pumped the air then retreated to the kitchen to get his own bowl. Soon they were snuggled onto the couch together, watching reruns over bowls of steaming chili. And Lissa was doing her best not to think about the infuriating man she'd seen that afternoon.

Chapter Ten

The search for a face for *Gamers* was starting to feel hopeless.

Grant sighed heavily as he stacked yet another resume in the "not interested" file. Ethan sat at the conference table with him, reclined in his chair, one ankle crossed over his knee, fingers of one hand tapping a rhythm on the oak. "Still nothing?" he asked.

Grant shoved the papers aside and ran his hands through his hair. "Nope."

Ethan wanted to avoid at all costs another conversation about him taking the role. "Maybe we can just abandon it for now—"

"You want to abandon an important part of our business plan? Really?" Grant rocked his chair, hands on the arms. "Ethan Talley wants to deviate from the business plan? What universe are we in?"

"I'm flexible," he muttered.

Grant scoffed. "You're as flexible as a fucking steel door, you liar."

"No, I'm realistic."

"All you're doing is avoiding talking about you taking this job, even though we both know you'd be the best person for it."

They were supposed to be friends, but lately Grant seemed like he was being puppet-mastered by Chloe. "It's starting to really piss me off lately how you think you seem to know what's best for me."

Grant narrowed his eyes, humor gone from his expression as his knuckles curled into a tight grip on his chair. "I've always been a pushy guy, so that's nothing new. And I have Chloe in my ear, telling me she's still worried about you. So you know what? Yes, I do think the best thing for you is to put yourself out there again. To see that there is a wider world than your little narrow worldview of pain and guilt."

Anger surged through Ethan in a white-hot flare as he slammed his hand down on the table. "How dare you?"

Grant stood up abruptly, sending his chair rolling backwards. "I'm so overstepping right now, that I can't even see the line. I know that. But know that I'm doing it because I love Chloe and goddamnit, I love you, too, even though you're a grumpy bastard. I wish you could see you how we all see you now. You choose to define yourself by what you did years ago. By one mistake—"

"It wasn't just one fucking mistake, Grant. Calling the death of my sister a mistake trivializes the whole thing—"

"What happened was nothing short of a tragedy," Grant said, tugging on his hair. "But you continuing to live in misery is a choice. A choice you make every day. A choice you force us to witness over and over and over again. Chloe is still here and she wants her big brother."

Ethan's chest tightened and he swore he was having a panic attack. "She has me."

Grant shook his head, his shoulders sagging. "She has this broken version of you. Which isn't fair to you or her."

Ethan turned his head away, staring out the large windows of the conference room. He didn't know what to say and he had no desire to listen to Grant anymore. Chloe was a sore spot for him, as his only sibling left. He worked so hard after Samantha's death to be there for Chloe, to protect her. He'd failed once already, not knowing she was placing the fixing of their broken family on her shoulders.

"She doesn't need you to do anything but be Ethan and be happy," Grant said quietly. "You don't have to worry about her. But you have to understand she loves you. If you didn't have people that cared about you, everyone would just leave you alone. So think about that. We're a pain in your ass because we care."

Ethan didn't answer and heard Grant huff out a breath before leaving. Ethan was alone in the conference room, and he might even be the only one in the whole office at this time on a Friday afternoon.

He didn't move, though. He didn't make an effort to go after Grant; instead he sat in the conference room and brooded.

And man, he was tired of brooding. He was tired of being a miserable bastard whose sister had to hound him to make him act like a human.

The only reason lately he'd felt like he had something to live for was his job, his sister, and…Lissa.

And he'd fucked that up. Around her, he wasn't the former E-Rad. He wasn't the scarred Ethan Talley. He was… Ethan. Just a guy. A guy who made her laugh, who made her come. Just a guy.

He'd let his own issues invade their time at the park and he'd lashed out at her. He wanted to let the whole thing go. Time would heal everything over, and eventually she'd barely remember him.

But the thought of her thinking he used her, him knowing he hadn't treated her well, soured his stomach. She hadn't deserved that. She hadn't asked for one single thing from him except what he asked of her. And he'd still treated her like she would want more.

So even though he knew he should let it go, he couldn't. He had to see her one last time, to tell her that she'd made him happy for a brief moment. That when she was in his arms, he hadn't thought about all the reasons he hated himself.

He still didn't quite understand what she was getting out of this arrangement, but she hadn't turned him away yet. That was the thing with Lissa—in the short time he'd known her—he believed what she said. He believed that what she was thinking would come out of her mouth. That she wouldn't hold back. That she'd call him out on being an asshole but then fucked with all the passion she possessed.

He had grown infatuated with her without even realizing it. How had that happened? And most of all, how the hell was he going to apologize?

. . .

Lissa's legs ached as she made her way to her car in the darkened parking lot. Every time she worked an event, she told herself over and over again not to lock her knees when she was standing. And to take some ibuprofen. She always forgot.

The charity event had been for the Willow Park Historical Society. It was a nonprofit, so she'd greatly reduced her rate. They'd plied her with food in thanks, and those little beef sliders had been delicious.

As she gazed up into the star-filled sky, her thoughts turned to Ethan, as they always had since that afternoon in the park. It'd been two weeks, and although she hadn't expected to hear from Ethan, it still stung.

She wished she knew his story, so she could make him

happy for longer than what it took him to come. There was a reason he wasn't the charming E-Rad anymore. She'd always been a curious woman, and Ethan was her focus right now.

She needed to get over it. She'd make her project work without him, because she knew now she could never approach him to ask for the favor. Even in Rona's name. Ethan needed to be respected, and they were both too affected by what had happened to remain impartial.

He'd accused her of using him, and she couldn't let him think that.

Her phone rang, and she dug in her purse until she pulled out the device. She didn't bother glancing at the caller ID, assuming it was Angel. "Hello?"

There was a pause, then a voice so deep, it was a rumble. "Lissa."

She stopped walking and blinked at the darkness in front of her. "Ethan?"

Another pause. "How are you?"

"I'm fine. Just leaving an event I was shooting."

"Oh." His voice was softer now. "I'm sure you're tired then, I won't—"

"Wait!" She held a hand out, even though he couldn't see her. "Wait. Why are you calling? I'll decide if I'm tired enough." Her last sentence held a bit of an attitude, and she cringed.

He exhaled into the phone. "I wanted to apologize for… shit."

There was a rustling, like he was rubbing his face. Lissa shuffled her feet. "Ethan?"

"Yes."

"Do you want to meet?"

More rustling then. "Only if you're not too tired from work—"

"I wouldn't have suggested it if I didn't want to do it."

There was a smile in his voice when he said, "Right. Of

course."

"Where do you want to meet?"

"Are you comfortable coming to my house? The dead bodies buried in my basement barely smell at all."

Lissa laughed. "Wow, an Ethan Talley original joke. I feel special."

"Don't get used to it. I won't spoil you with my amazing sense of humor."

"I'll come over."

"Okay."

"Text me the address. I'm leaving now."

"Okay, drive safe." And then the line went dead.

Lissa stared at her phone for a minute, biting her lip. This was probably a bad idea. She'd go over there, they'd have sex, and then he'd probably turn cold again. At first, it'd been all physical. She wanted him, he wanted her, and their chemistry was great. She would have been fine to keep it to strictly hookups, but now that she'd seen more of Ethan, her fix-it gene was kicking in. Which wasn't really fair. Ethan probably didn't want to be fixed and surely not by some random woman he slept with a couple of times.

She sighed. There was no sense in wasting a really good hair day on a bunch of guests who didn't pay attention to the camera lady in the corner. After a decade of weaves, she'd gone natural about two years ago, and her short curls were on point today. At least she could see Ethan on a day she looked fabulous.

So she got in her car, programmed her GPS to the address he texted, and began to drive.

His house was a large colonial set all by its lonesome at the end of a cul-de-sac. The perimeter was marked with tall tress, so his house wasn't visible to his neighbors. She wasn't surprised. Not one bit.

After parking in his driveway, she pulled her camera bag

out of the car with her. No matter how private his house was, she never left her camera equipment alone. That was her livelihood.

She wore a plain T-shirt, a pair of jeans, and flat sneakers. She felt frumpy, but she hadn't planned to be summoned by Ethan Talley.

She knocked, and when he opened the door, her mouth went dry. She sure wasn't thinking about her clothes anymore. He wore a pair of gray sweatpants low on his hips, bare feet, and a faded Phillies T-shirt.

So, it was confirmed, Ethan looked just as delicious in lounge clothes as he did in a formal suit. What a jerk.

When she was able to drag her eyes away from the rather large bulge in his crotch, she met his eyes. "Hey."

His gaze traveled down to her feet and back up. "Did you make it okay?"

She nodded. "Sure, easy to find."

He stepped back so she could walk past him. He gestured to her bag. "Want me to take that?"

"Oh"—she handed it to him—"sure, you can put it anywhere. I never leave my camera unattended."

With a flush, she remembered their last encounter. He must have, too, because he ducked his head and placed her camera bag on a hook in the front closet door. "Right."

"Ethan—"

"Would you like a drink?"

His gaze told her he needed time—that he didn't want to delve into the apologies and the talking right away. She could handle that. So she smiled. "Sure."

"Water, beer, chardonnay?"

She followed him into the living room. "Chardonnay would be great, please."

He directed her to the couch. "I'll be right back." And then he headed out toward the kitchen.

She eyed the couch but decided to stay standing. The room was neat, clean, and organized. Several pictures were on his mantle, and she walked over to peer at them. In one, Ethan stood with his arms around two women. There were enough similarities to assume they were related, if not siblings. Ethan wasn't scarred in that picture. In fact, he looked just like she remembered E-Rad looking. Happy and charming and loving life.

As Ethan walked back into the living room, holding two wine glasses, she was struck again with how much he'd changed.

She took a glass from him and then took a sip, eyeing him as he held his glass with his large hand, brow furrowed as he stared at a point on the wall over her shoulder. His shoulders were tense, his lips thinned.

"Look, I'm sorry for how I acted when I last saw you." He still wasn't meeting her eyes, but she stayed silent. "That was wrong of me. I'm surprised you agreed to come here today. I'm clearly not a whole man, and you've put up with my moods numerous times now…" He blew out a breath and finally met her gaze. "I know the sex is great, but you didn't sign up to deal with me."

She glanced to the side, her gaze resting on the picture, and when she turned to him, his eyes had followed hers. And instead of the frown that had marred his features, now there was…something else in his expression. Something painful and heavy, and it nearly took her breath away.

She gripped the wine glass tighter. This was a moment that could change their arrangement. If she admitted she knew who he was, he could throw her out. He could be angry. He could rage and tell her she was a liar.

Or he could open up. And maybe, she'd have a chance to get a peek at the soft inner core of Ethan Talley. Just the fact that he stood in front of her, not taking care to mask his features, gave her hope.

She took another gulp of wine, grimacing as the alcohol slid down her throat, then she blurted, "I know who you are."

His whole body jerked so hard she thought he'd lose his balance. He didn't correct his face or hide his shock as he stared at her. "Excuse me?" His voice was a whisper.

Lissa squared her shoulders to gather her courage. "I know who you are. You're E-Rad. I knew it from the moment I heard your voice. My brother and I... We used to watch you all the time when we were younger."

He didn't move. He didn't even blink.

"I didn't tell you because that wasn't what we had. We didn't do anything but take each others' clothes off. I'm not sure what we are anymore, but we feel past that. Hell, we already had our first fight, right?" She tried for levity, but he didn't move a smile, not even a quirk of his lips. Taking a step closer, she placed her wine glass on the coffee table. "Ethan? Can you please say something?"

Finally, he blinked. Once. Twice. Then he swallowed slowly. When his gaze returned to that far-off point over her shoulder, she knew she'd lost him.

She'd gone too far.

Without emotion, he said, "I'd like you to leave now."

She didn't want to, not at all, not when his face was deathly pale, those scars standing out in livid streaks along his neck and jaw. But he wasn't there anymore; he was somewhere else, somewhere he dwelled on that pain. Somewhere she couldn't touch.

So with what dignity she had left, she walked to the hall closet and gathered her bags. With her hand on the doorknob, she turned around once more to see he hadn't moved. "This is your house, and I'm respecting your wishes. But you have to know, Ethan, I don't want to leave. You have stories. Well I have stories, too. I have scars just like you, but mine aren't on my skin. I think you would have found we could have dulled each others' pain. But if you're not interested, then neither am I."

She opened the door and walked out.

Chapter Eleven

Ethan stared at his mantle, at the pictures he kept there to torture himself, with Lissa's words ringing in his head. It took gargantuan effort to tear himself away from his own misery to think about what she said.

Yes, his initial attraction to Lissa had been all physical. But she made him laugh. He enjoyed her company and listening to her talk. And she was so beautiful when she was focused on her work, like that day in the park.

Would it kill him to let her in? Just a little? It was his mental defect that had been the reason they'd parted ways poorly at the park.

He could head down his hallway and make himself a cocoon on his bed for days. Or he could see if there was any way Lissa could ease some of the pain he'd been carrying for years.

We could have dulled each others' pain.

What was hiding behind her large smile and warm eyes? What kind of pain had she known? The sound of her car starting outside tore him out of his thoughts, and before he could stop himself, he ran out of the house, leaping down the stairs of his front porch and toward Lissa's car. Her head was down, most likely changing gears so she could back out of his driveway and leave him.

Like he'd told her to do. He was such an asshole.

The headlights blinding him, he slammed his hands down on the hood of her car, and her head jerked up. He couldn't see her expression well, so he waited to see if the car would move. He wasn't sure how long they stared at each other before her arm lowered and the car shut off.

By the time his eyes adjusted to the dark again, she stood in the open doorway of her car.

She didn't say one word. And it wasn't because she didn't have words. It was because it was his turn to talk. To explain. He knew that.

He curled his hands into fists where they still rested on her hood. He held her gaze, even though he wanted to look away, then he gave her the sole reason he was scarred and pissed off and alone. "I killed my sister."

She didn't move. Her jaw twitched like she meant to say something, then she shook her head and walked toward him. She reached out, tugged on one of his hands, threaded her fingers through it, and led him back into the house.

He followed her, thankful she hadn't left. That those four words hadn't sent her running for the hills.

He'd left the front door open in his wake, and she walked inside, once again placing her camera back on the hook inside the closet door, along with her purse. In the living room, she pushed on his shoulders until he sat on the couch, then she handed him his wineglass and picked up hers.

The whole time, his mind spun as he tried to read her expression. Lissa was expressive, but right now, she was frustratingly blank.

When she sat beside him and placed a hand on his knee,

she nodded.

That was his cue to talk. He thought for a split second about backing out, but it was too late. So he licked his lips and spilled his guts. "I had a lot of money when I was commentating video games. One of the things I bought was a flashy car. I was showing off, with my sister in the passenger seat, and I lost control. We crashed. She didn't survive, and I emerged like this." He gestured toward his face and neck. "Sure, I'm vain, and the scars bother me sometimes, but mostly it's what they represent. They are an everyday reminder that because of me, my sister is no longer here. I took her from our other sister, from her parents, from her family and friends. Everyone loved Samantha. And because of me, we're all without her." He shook his head. "And don't tell me, 'oh it was an accident, it wasn't your fault' or any of that other well-meaning bullshit. Because I know it all, and it doesn't matter. It doesn't. I caused her death, and everyone knows it. But most of all me."

He ran out of steam and let his head fall back on the couch. He rolled it to the side to see if Lissa was horrified or sympathetic. He wasn't sure he wanted to see either reaction. He didn't even want to be having this conversation.

She stood up and walked to the mantel, then picked up the photo of him, Samantha, and Chloe. "Which one is Samantha?"

"The one on the right," he said, closing his eyes. He could recount that picture completely from memory, the way her hair was blown out to one side in the breeze. The hole in her jeans on her right knee.

"She was very pretty," Lissa said. "And that smile… She looks like someone I would have been friends with."

He opened his eyes to see her gazing at the picture with affection. "She would have liked you a lot. And you would have liked her."

She placed the picture back on the mantel and turned

to look at him, crossing her arms over her chest and leaning against the wall. "So what does this have to do with what happened at the park?"

"You were looking at my scars," he said. "And all I could think about was that I couldn't give you more. I wasn't capable of it. I've spent my life since the accident avoiding people and…avoiding everything, really. I'm either here, or with my other sister, or at work. I didn't want to have this conversation."

She cocked her head. "And now that we're having it, how do you feel?"

He smiled a little at that. "Okay, I guess."

"I mean, you're still breathing. No heart attack. Blood still pumping. It's amazing what we're capable of."

If anyone else had said that to him, he would have told them to fuck off. But she wasn't mocking. She was watching him like she understood. Like she knew how much this was taking out of him. "Where are your scars?" he asked softly.

She bit her lip and looked away before meeting his eyes again. "My scar is in Willow Park Cemetery, and it's in the shape of a headstone for my sister."

He sat up and braced his forearms on his knees, waiting for her to keep talking.

She ran her hand up and down one thigh, the sound of her nails catching on the denim rhythmic. "So, my sister was in a one-car accident. Rona was coming home late from class and fell asleep. The accident left her with burn scars similar to yours, but she was never the same. The accident triggered something, and we all missed a lot of warning signs. She, um, killed herself a couple of years ago."

His heart plummeted. "Oh, Lissa, I'm so sorry."

She met his gaze directly. "Thanks. I am, too." She took a step toward him. "You're not the only one with guilt. I didn't cause her accident, but I didn't take care of her afterward. I didn't pay enough attention, and I missed everything. I wasn't there for my sister when she needed me the most, and now she's not here."

He stared at his hands as he twisted them. "I don't know how to make this guilt go away. I tried at first but then I decided I'd have to learn to live with it. But it's killing me slowly." He hadn't admitted that to anyone before, not even Chloe. Not even himself.

There was a rustle of clothes and then Lissa was on her knees in front of him, peering up into his face. She reached out slowly and brushed back the hair that had fallen off his forehead. "I think...we have to forgive ourselves. But damn if I haven't figured out how to do that."

He smiled, although it felt wobbly. "Yeah, I don't have the golden ticket for that."

"Does it help that I tell you I understand? I know our situations aren't the same, but—"

He shook his head. "They're not, but it does help. This isn't the conversation I expected to have, or wanted to have, but it might be the conversation I needed. What about you?"

"I hate that you had to go through what you did, and that you still face it every day, but yeah, talking about this has helped."

He reached out and drew her further into the V of his legs. She braced her hands on his thighs and peered up into his face as he rubbed a thumb along her jaw. "Will you stay tonight? I don't know...I don't know what I can promise. I'm pretty fucked up, Lissa. But I can promise tonight."

She didn't even hesitate before she nodded. "Yes, I'll stay."

• • •

By the time they made it to the bedroom, fused at the mouth, the slow pace of the evening had morphed into something frenzied.

It was like after a controlled conversation where they were forced to humanize themselves to each other, now all they wanted was to get out a pure animal lust.

Lissa still couldn't believe Ethan had followed her outside. She'd sworn that was the end of it all, but then he'd flown out of his house like a blue-eyed bat and stood like a statue in front of her car.

And his aching voice saying the words—*I killed my sister*—would stick with her forever.

But she'd dwell on that another time, because right now, Ethan was unbuttoning her jeans and slipping his hands down the back of them to palm her ass. He tugged her to him, and she smashed against him with a grunt, her fingernails digging into his skin, since he'd already shed his shirt.

She tilted her head back as his lips coasted down her neck, nipping along the way. He tugged her shirt off her shoulder, and his lips felt so good she didn't even protest that he was stretching it out.

She reached down and palmed the bulge in his sweatpants. "This for me?" she asked as he leaned back to pull her shirt over her head.

"What do you think?" he growled, focusing his attention on her breasts.

She gasped as he unsnapped her bra and the cool air hit her hard nipples. "I think I've been a good girl, and this is for me."

He smiled then, a devilishly wicked smile. "Good answer."

He shoved her gently, and she fell back onto the bed. He took off her shoes, kissing the inside of her ankles, then slid her jeans down her hips and off onto the floor. His hands skimmed over her knees, up her thighs, his eyes bright as he took in her nearly naked body.

She squirmed under his touch as his thumbs skimmed the

edges of her panties. He stared up at her, a challenge in his eyes as he slid her underwear down her legs, and then slowly, one-by-one, he lifted her legs onto his shoulders as he knelt beside the bed. His gaze was between her legs now, and she sucked in a breath as he slid a finger down her wet flesh. He rubbed it over her opening, back and forth over her clit, as she gasped, rising up onto her elbows to watch what he was doing. "Are you going to put your mouth on me, or just look at it?" she asked.

He smiled. "You want my mouth?"

"I want your tongue on my clit and your fingers inside me, that's what I want. And after that, I want you to take off those tempting sweatpants, get your cock out, and fuck me."

He grinned and laughed. "There's no one like you, you know that?"

She shuddered as he circled her opening. "I know; I have a dirty mouth."

He leaned down and blew a stream of cold air on her clit. "Hmmm, yeah it is dirty, but I like it."

He flattened his tongue and ran it over her in one long, slow lick. She let her head fall back as he worked her over with his tongue, spearing it into her, then pulling back to swirl it over her clit. He held her open with his thumbs, and just when she was about to holler about needing to be filled, he shoved two fingers inside of her.

She cried out. Loudly. So loud that he jerked up, eyes wide. "Damn, I'm glad my neighbors aren't close."

"No talking," she panted as he thrust his fingers in and out. "Your mouth should not be talking right now, it should be doing things that will make me come." He bit her inner thigh and she yelped, which turned into laughter. "Fuck, okay I'm sorry."

"Bossy," he muttered, but then he did as she asked and his mouth was back on her and his fingers were working her inside and fuck this was heaven. She ran her hands through his dark hair as he worked her open. When he crooked his fingers and found something inside of her, her orgasm rocketed through her with no warning. None at all. She couldn't even warn him as she ground onto his face, noises leaving her throat as she collapsed onto her back, unable to continue supporting herself.

"Oh my God," she moaned, unable to move as Ethan arranged her limbs lengthwise on the bed. A condom wrapper crinkled, and then he was between her legs, notching his cock at her entrance and then shoving home in one thrust. She wrapped her arms and legs around him, her face in his neck, as he fucked her.

"I'm not going to last long," he said in her ear. "Not when you looked like a fucking queen coming on my mouth. Not when I can still taste you on my tongue. And I already want more."

She reached down and squeezed his ass, his words doing something to heal her heart. She wanted to do the same for him.

"Best I ever had." She told the truth. "I knew you could work that cock of yours, but now that I know you can do the same with your finger and tongue, I might never let you out of this bed."

His hips stuttered, and with a soft groan, he came.

She wanted to say, *I love how you treat my body, but will you treat my heart the same?* Instead, she closed her eyes and held him close.

Chapter Twelve

At rest, Ethan looked years younger. It was apparent, now, how much tension he carried around every waking minute of the day. Because asleep, his skin was smooth, his mouth no longer set in a grim line.

His lips were curled slightly, his hands clutching the pillow she'd slept on. She thought about last night, when she'd detangled herself from his embrace to retrieve her silk headscarf she always kept in her purse. His eyes were open when she'd come back to bed with the floral fabric wrapped around her hair to protect it. She'd wondered if he'd make a comment, because her spare scarf wasn't exactly glamorous. But he'd smiled and gently swiped his fingers along the material above her ear, then he'd closed his eyes and was asleep again in seconds.

Watching him as he slept in this morning, she rubbed her chest at the ache there, thinking that this could be the Ethan everyone saw, if only he let go of the guilt. If only he saw himself the way she saw him.

Carefully, she padded from the bedroom, retrieved her

camera from the hall closet, and tip-toed back. He hadn't moved an inch. She dug her camera out of her bag and fiddled around with the settings before holding it up to her face and squinting in the viewfinder.

This was where Lissa was most comfortable. This was how she communicated, through her pictures. This would be how she showed him he deserved happiness. She clicked a couple of pictures of his sleeping form and then paused, waiting for him to wake up. His nose twitched, and she covered her mouth to stifle a laugh as he settled again.

She held out her hand above him and snapped some photos blind for another angle. She took all kinds of shots all around the room in different light. When her shutter fell silent, she breathed deeply. Then she packed up her camera and put it back in the hall closet. She'd go home, study and edit them, and show him the best pictures of himself. She wasn't sure he'd appreciate waking up to a camera ambush.

After a quick trip to the bathroom to remove her scarf, she walked back into the bedroom to see ice-blue eyes open and alert. He hadn't moved, but he tracked her as she crossed the room and climbed into bed beside him.

His body was like a furnace, especially when he wrapped an arm around her waist and tugged her against him.

He hadn't spoken yet, so she didn't speak, either, instead allowing him to cocoon her in the warmth of his body and the sheets. They were both still naked from the night before, and while watching his eyes for a flinch, she ran her fingers over the scars along his neck and shoulder. He didn't move at all, and as she went lower, her palms sliding on unmarked skin, she saw he was hard.

She wrapped her hands around it and stroked. His hips jerked, and his lips parted.

"Do you want me to take care of this?" she asked, skimming her lips over his jaw. He opened his mouth as if to talk, but instead nodded. She stroked him again and then stopped. "I will if you agree to go out to breakfast with me."

He immediately frowned and his eyes blazed. She already missed his peaceful expression. "Excuse me?"

"Breakfast, then video games."

His frown grew deeper until it was a mammoth groove in his forehead. "Are you blackmailing me?"

She didn't want to hole up in his apartment, which he'd said he'd been doing for years. She wanted him to get out and enjoy life. "Yes, I am."

"You are an evil witch." She let go of his cock, and he groaned. "No…"

"Then promise me we can go out for sausage gravy and biscuits."

He made a face of disgust. "No."

"No?"

"I will not eat that. I'll order something proper, like an omelet."

She grinned and wrapped her fingers around his shaft again then nuzzled her nose into his neck. "So is that a yes?"

"It's a yes," he mumbled as his hand skimmed her naked hip. "No changing the terms on me. Breakfast, then video games."

She pressed an open-mouthed kiss to the skin of his neck, where it was scarred. He didn't even notice, because she was stroking him at the same time. "Okay," she whispered.

With a stretch, she reached for a condom from his bedside table, opening the package, and then rolled it down his cock. He was breathing hard, his abs flexing as he lay on his back and watched her.

She rose up onto her knees, straddled him, and slowly sheathed him with herself. His eyes fell closed on a moan as she sat fully onto him. His hands fluttered at her hips before settling at her thighs, his thumbs digging into her skin. "Lissa."

She bit her lip, because even though they'd had sex last night, he was still a lot to handle, especially in this position. But damn he felt good, and he felt even better as she began to rock her hips.

He watched her with his lips parted, eyes half lidded. "So beautiful."

She braced herself on his chest and ground onto him harder. She could change the angle in this position, so the head of his cock hit her just right. He helped, too, as his thumbs drifted between her legs and rubbed her clit. She wondered what she looked like.

When she came, he wasn't far behind, and he rolled them gently onto their sides before pulling out and disposing of the condom.

She reached up and brushed his hair out of his eyes, and he greeted her action with a small smile. "I don't know if this is good for me."

"If what's good for you?"

"Getting used to this. Last night and this morning have been some of the best I've had in years. When are you going to realize there is a man out there for you who smiles more and laughs all the time and enjoys going out in public?"

Oh, be still her heart. She shook her head. "Maybe that's not what I want." He scoffed, but she wasn't done. "No, you don't get to tell me what I want and what I don't want. First of all, I haven't had the desire to spend time with anyone in a while. I live with my brother, and I work, and I'm happy with that. I'm fine being alone. So you have to understand that I'm choosing to be with you. Every time we've seen each other, I never felt like I couldn't say no. You've respected me then, so respect me now to know that I have my own mind. If I didn't want to be here, I wouldn't fucking be here." When she was finished, she was breathing hard and that was definitely a rant she'd gone on. She winced, hoping Ethan didn't take offense, but instead, after a brief pause, where he did nothing but blink at her, he smiled. A large, E-Rad-reminiscent smile.

He pressed a kiss to her lips. "I don't believe in fate or any of that bullshit, but, Lissa, you were sent to me for some reason. Most people take a look at my scars and my scowls and they placate me. You don't do that. You tell me the truth, and you don't sugarcoat, and fuck, but you're a breath of fresh air."

She ducked her head, her cheeks heating. "There've been men who didn't like my honesty or bluntness. Or bossiness."

He cupped her cheek, his expression tender. "Those weren't men. Those were boys, and they didn't know what a gem you are."

Tears threatened, but she blinked them back. What if she or someone had said that to Rona. Would she still be alive today? Pushing back the stab of guilt, she rose up on an elbow. "Okay, so you ready for your breakfast now?"

He hesitated for a second, still studying her face, then nodded. "Sure, let's get on with it.

• • •

Ethan stared at Lissa's plate, which was covered with an off-white goopy mess. "That looks like someone ate a steak and drank a gallon of milk and then vomited it up onto a plate."

She paused with the fork halfway to her mouth, then she dropped it back down and pointed a finger at him. "You will not ruin this breakfast for me. You're just jealous because you ordered a whole plate of bland."

"It does not taste bland."

"It's an egg white omelet! Who eats stuff like that?"

He shoved a forkful in his mouth and mumbled, "Me."

She raised an eyebrow then picked up her utensil and resumed eating. She made an exaggerated moaning sound as she chewed. He shook his head, unable to hide his smile.

"You want some?" she asked.

"What *is* it?"

She huffed out a breath. "How can you live in Pennsylvania and not have had sausage gravy and biscuits?"

"Probably because it looks like vomit."

"Quit saying that."

He pressed his lips together.

"So it's gravy with bits of sausage in it and they pour it over biscuits. I like it with a lot of pepper."

He took a sip of his coffee. "I like it on your plate and not mine."

She laughed, the sound of it warming him more than coffee ever could. "Fine, be like that. I'm just happy you're here."

He leaned forward and cleared his throat. "Me, too."

She smiled and dug back in to her plate.

He was happy, too. After the night they had, where he'd spilled his guts, he hadn't expected this to be the outcome. Them laughing over breakfast after several rounds of really good sex.

Despite the loss of her sister, Lissa was full of life, and patient, and so brutally honest he finally stopped guessing if she had ulterior motives. She actually wanted to spend time with his grumpy ass.

Part of him knew what she was doing—getting him to get out of the house. He'd told her he rarely ventured out. But while it irritated him when Grant did it and concerned him when Chloe did it—when Lissa did it…he appreciated it just a little. That might not have been fair to Grant and Chloe, but he couldn't help how he felt.

Lissa did it for him. In bed and out. He wouldn't have passed up seeing her face light up as she ate her breakfast or her polite smile while she thanked their waitress.

It felt natural to come out to breakfast with her. He'd expected to be so ill at ease he couldn't eat, but he'd managed to scrape his plate and was now on his second cup of coffee.

When Lissa pushed her mostly empty plate away and rubbed her stomach, he laughed softly. "Had enough?"

"Oh, I'm going to need to do some extra cardio after that meal."

He tapped his chin with a finger. "Hmm, I happen to know a really great cardio plan."

She hesitated then lifted a corner of her mouth. "Oh yeah?"

"It involves no clothes and typically some sort of penetration."

She sputtered. "I knew that was coming, and it still made me laugh."

"Well, there aren't many where that came from, so don't get used to it."

She rolled her eyes and took a sip from her coffee mug. She set it on the table and wrapped her hands around it, then tapped a ring on her right hand on the ceramic. "So, what's your sister like?"

The unspoken, "the one who's still alive" hung in the air between them.

Ethan swallowed and debated whether he wanted to talk about this. Lissa didn't give him an out, didn't say, "Only if you want to talk." She stared at him steadily and waited. He blew out a breath. "Her name's Chloe. She's a software debugger, which means she pokes holes in the software security so companies know where the problems are. She's really smart and has the biggest heart. She's engaged to Grant, whom you met." She nodded. "And she's very, very happy. And that's all I ever wanted for her, was to be happy. She took the death of Samantha hard, like we all did. My parents and I had a falling out, and Chloe put a lot of that on her shoulders, thinking she needed to get us all back together." He shook his head. "But that's not her responsibility, to keep our family together. It was blasted apart, and I don't think it will ever be put back together the way it was."

Lissa hadn't taken her eyes off him. "Of course it won't be put back together the way it was. There's a piece missing. It's all about finding a new normal. A new way to talk to one another and understand triggers."

Lissa had a way of speaking that didn't make Ethan bristle. Her words weren't a lecture; they were a shared experience. He shifted in his seat and cocked his head. "How so?"

She blinked, as if she hadn't expected him to respond favorably. "After Rona died, we all blamed ourselves, I think. When she was alive, we all thought the other was watching her, and in the end, none of us had been giving her what she needed. We didn't want to make the same mistake twice. We didn't want to let one another down, so we closed ranks." She broke for a sip of coffee. Her hands trembled slightly as she placed the mug back on the table. "We were all hurting and it wasn't easy, but we made sure we spoke. We stayed honest with one another about how we felt. My brother and I moved in together. We were both between leases, so it worked out. We see my parents every week for dinner. It's not always easy, but we're committed." She gazed at him. "What happened between you and your parents?"

He swallowed, the thought of his parents causing a flare of pain between his eyes like it always did. "I blamed myself, and they blamed me, too. Instead of working on the relationship, I shoved them away further. I think…I think it's mostly my fault, the chasm that's there now. And at this point, I'm not sure it's fixable."

"Do you want to fix it?"

"Of course. My parents have flaws, like everyone, but they are good parents. And they don't deserve this broken family.

That I caused."

She shook her head. "I'll tell you now, they're not going to forgive you until you forgive yourself. I believe that with all my heart. If you come to them like this, they'll see you exactly how you see yourself, and I'm sure that will be painful to them. They lost a daughter, and now they lost you. You see that, right?"

He did, but it was easier said than done. He rubbed his forehead, trying to soothe away throbbing pain. Dredging up all of this was exhausting. It was why he avoided talking about it and why he hadn't gone to therapy.

Lissa reached across the table and squeezed his hand. "I think that was enough deep thought for the morning, don't you?"

He was grateful for her perception. He cleared his throat and clasped his hands on the table in front of him. "Yeah, I, uh, think I need to shoot some things on screen now."

She laughed. "Video games it is then."

Chapter Thirteen

The breakfast conversation lingered in the background as they played *Aric's Revenge* back at Ethan's house. At first, Lissa had worried she'd overstepped, pressed too hard. But while Ethan was subdued, he seemed thoughtful.

As time went on, he loosened up a little more, talking to himself about the game, and she swore she was in the same room as E-Rad. Well, she *was* in the same room as E-Rad, just an older version.

She liked this one better.

The current E-Rad spoke with less bravado and more facts. Showed off less and analyzed more. He spoke about the game's patches, how they improved play, and how to get the most out of the game.

He was so fascinating to listen to that she was barely paying attention to her own player and walked in front of Ethan's dragon just as he flamed up a house. And her with it. "Oops," she said with a wince. "That's no good."

"Lissa," Ethan growled.

"What?"

"You offed yourself! Pay attention."

"I am paying attention."

He shot her a look.

"I am! I'm paying attention to you, because you're more interesting than this video game."

His fingers stopped moving and they stared at the screen as a house burned. He didn't look at her as he spoke. "My sister said my inner E-Rad was re-emerging."

"She's right, but this is E-Rad 2.0. A more mature version. I like you better now. You got on my nerves sometimes before."

He turned to her slowly with a grin. "Oh yeah? Tell me please."

She tapped her fingers on the controller. "You used to do that pistol thing. When you killed a main guy. It was pompous."

"Pompous?" his voice rose.

"Pompous. And your winking was sleazy."

He threw back his head and laughed. "I happened to like my wink."

"Sleazy," she repeated.

He tossed his controller to the side and rose from his spot on the floor. Lissa fell onto her back on the couch as he climbed over her. With a quick flick of his fingers, the button on her jeans was undone, then her zipper was down, and his hand was inside of her panties.

She arched her back and moaned as a finger pressed against her. He licked his lips and gazed down her body. "Sleazy, huh? Is this sleazy?"

She gripped the armrest behind her with both hands and bit her lip as he dipped a finger inside of her. "Shit, Ethan."

"I love how you respond to me. Right now, you're panting already, spreading your legs as far as you can because you know I'll make you feel good. You know I'll make you come so hard on this couch that you see stars."

She cried out as another finger joined the first. The heel of his palm pressed against her clit as he leaned down and nipped at her jaw. "One touch and you're so wet for me. You want to know what makes me happy, Lissa? This. You. And me. Breakfast and video games and my fingers deep inside of you. That's what makes me happy. This is fucking living."

She gasped as he pressed harder, thrusting his fingers in and out of her, his thumb now stroking her clit. "This makes me happy, too," she said breathlessly.

His lips were at her ear now. "I'd be even happier if you came. I'm going to watch you, memorize every emotion on your face, every sound you make."

She reached down and gripped his wrist, grinding against his hand as she felt the orgasm start. "Oh shit."

He pulled back immediately, those blue-flame eyes on her. "That's it. Come for me."

She didn't need the command, because it was already starting. Staring up at him, the orgasm rocketed through her, a fire that spread out to every limb. When she collapsed back onto the couch with a slump, panting, Ethan's fingers were still inside of her. He pulled them out slowly, and without looking away, sucked them into his mouth. She watched as he licked them then leaned down and took her mouth in a hot, wet kiss.

When he pulled back, there was a smirk on his lips. She reached for his pants, but he jerked back. "I'm okay."

She frowned. "But you're hard, and I need to do something to pay you back for that amazing orgasm."

He laughed softly. "You've already paid me back. And this…this feels good. To want. I want to keep wanting for a little while longer."

She understood that. Boy she did. So she nodded. "Okay."

He slid back down to the floor, adjusting himself with a grimace. Then he picked up his controller. "Want to play a little longer?"

She took a deep breath. "Okay, I'll try not to get burned up this time."

He grinned.

Later that afternoon, Lissa sat with her knees under her chin, clicking through the pictures she'd taken of Ethan that morning. She hadn't told him yet because she wanted time to look through them, choosing the best ones. She didn't plan to touch them up in any way other than color correcting and fixing some lighting issues. It was important to her that Ethan see these raw images.

His smile when they parted ways that morning was so much lighter than she'd ever seen it. It rattled her how much she cared and how much he'd wormed his way into her heart.

Her project would be completely without him. After what they went through, and the future she was increasingly desiring with him, she didn't want to approach him about it. She'd tell him after she showed him the snapshots.

On the screen now was one of the pictures she'd taken blindly, the camera held at arm's length over his still body. She knew this was a little creepy, but she'd done it. And she was determined to show them to him. She wished she would have done this for Rona—taken pictures and let Rona see her how everyone else saw her.

A picture was more than a picture. Her shots were the way she saw the world, the way she saw the subject of the photo. They were a snapshot in time and from *her* lens.

As her gaze traveled over the way the light caressed his face, the smooth planes of his skin, and the mottled scars, all she saw was the beauty of Ethan. He was a man who felt his scars more inside than outside, and she hoped she was doing something, even if only a little, to help him heal.

He was going to have to do most of the painful process on his own.

"Who's that?"

A voice startled her; she dropped her legs to the floor and twisted in her chair, a hand at her chest. She blew out a breath when she spotted Angel standing in the doorway. "You scared the shit out of me. I didn't hear you come in."

He smiled and sank down on the edge of her bed. "You never do when you're working. So who's that?"

She bit her lip. "Uh, this is Ethan Talley. E-Rad."

Angel squinted to see the screen closer. "Really? You took pictures of him when he was asleep? Damn that's creepy."

She rolled her eyes and closed the photos, because it felt weird to have someone look at them, even if it was her brother. "Don't judge me."

"Did you have a good night?"

She squirmed as she rotated her chair to face him. "Yes."

He snickered. "So he agreed to be in your project?"

She shook her head. "No, I'm not asking him anymore."

"Why not?"

"Because I don't think it's right. Not now that we have this…relationship."

"It's a relationship now?"

She was barely sure herself. "I think so. We get along so well, and I think we make each other better people. He lost someone like we did, but he handled it completely different. He shut off rather than let his family in, you know?"

Angel's face was sober. "Shit."

"So he doesn't need to be placed in the public eye right now. I was thinking of my project first, before the human. And that's wrong. Humans come first."

Angel was silent for a moment. "You do think of people first, Lissa. That's why you're doing this project."

"I know, but—"

"You're thinking of who's involved and what this project means every step of the way. Don't be so hard on yourself."

She swallowed thickly as her eyes began to sting. "Okay."

He stood up and stretched. "So, you hungry?"

"I had sausage gravy and biscuits this morning, so I don't think I'll eat for two days."

"You ate that delicacy without me?" He pouted.

She laughed. "Give me a month to work off the calories from this morning and we'll go out for the same thing."

"Fine," he huffed. "I'm going to make a sandwich. "You okay?"

"Yep."

He gave her a wave and walked out.

She turned her chair back to her computer and opened up the beta site where she and Daniel were preparing the project before it went live. Ethan's pictures would look perfect in it, as they were taken in Lissa's portrait style. But it wasn't meant to be. Those pictures were for her, and for Ethan, too. He'd see soon that he was worth more than a scarred, grumpy hermit.

• • •

Ethan's finger hovered over the track pad. This was the fourth damn time today he'd tried to look at videos of himself and chickened out. He'd had so much coffee that he thought his finger might click on a video just from jittering.

Sunday was supposed to be a relaxing day for him, and instead he'd spent most of the morning pacing and guzzling caffeine.

He inhaled sharply, exhaled slowly, and pressed on the green arrow.

The sounds of shooting immediately filled his living room. And then, his own voice. "Hey, E-Rad here. Got some requests to play the new *Assassin's Creed*, and since Ubisoft was kind enough to send me a copy, I'm gonna show you all the tricks and shit, eh?"

E-Rad winked at the camera. Ethan winced. Damn, that *was* kind of sleazy.

But as Ethan watched E-Rad talk and move and make exaggerated noises as he slashed a bad guy's throat, he didn't seem like such a stranger anymore. Ethan *was* E-Rad. Treating that guy like a totally different person wasn't doing Ethan any favors at working to bring himself out of the trenches.

If he wanted to move on, if he wanted to get over this hump and be the kind of man who could stand next to Lissa with pride, then he had to do this. He had to see that, while he was older, he was still the same person. He could still be charming and outgoing and…maybe even handsome. He could still be a decent brother, lover, and maybe even a decent son again.

"I think this game is gonna be Top Dawg on the E-Rad scale, what do you think, guys?"

Ethan snorted a laugh. If he was going to do anything in front of the camera again, he was getting rid of the E-Rad name and any type of outdated lingo like Top Dawg. For fuck's sake.

He made a pistol shape with his fingers at E-rad on the screen and fired.

On Monday, Grant stormed in to Ethan's office and then closed the door behind him. Ethan lifted his head and watched the man pace a couple of times, his mouth twitching, before standing in front of his desk, hands on his hips. His face was red, his hair grooved from his fingers.

Ethan folded his hands on his desk in front of him and waited his friend out. He hadn't talked to Grant since their argument Friday. He knew his friend. He knew Grant would bust in here all blustered and unsure whether to keep yelling at Ethan or apologize.

Finally Grant opened his mouth and pointed a finger at Ethan. "You—!" He stopped abruptly and changed gears. "I'm sorry. For Friday. I know I said a lot of things I shouldn't have, but I thought about it over the weekend and I talked to Chloe about it, and I really think I wasn't too far off base. I don't think asking you to step up for this company is so bad. I'm not sorry for pushing the issue." He held up his hands. "But I'll back off now. I realize that getting in your face isn't what you need and I'm sorry for that. Sometimes I fuck up this friend and future brother-in-law thing, okay?"

Ethan nodded slowly, trying not to smile as Grant wore himself out. He must not have done a good job, because Grant narrowed his eyes and cocked his head. "Are you smiling?"

Ethan tugged down the corners of his lips. "No way."

Grant stepped closer. "No seriously, I think you were smiling."

"Certainly not. I take your apology seriously."

"Are you drunk?"

Ethan laughed. "What the hell? No, I'm not drunk."

"Then why are you being weird and agreeable and doing that weird thing with your lips? And laughing? What?"

"I don't know what you're talking about."

Grant gave him a look but then rolled his eyes. "I don't know what's going on with you, but I'll leave you alone now." He backed away toward the door. "I just… Yeah, I'm done nagging you, okay?"

"Good," Ethan said.

Grant placed his hand on the doorknob. "No more hounding you to get back in front of the camera."

"Excellent." He straightened some papers, and as Grant was one step out of his office, Ethan said. "Because I'm going to do it."

Grant froze. He didn't move for a good twenty seconds. Ethan knew because he counted. Then slowly, Grant walked backward, shut the office door again, and only then did he turn around.

His mouth was open, his wide eyes blinking. It took him a little longer before he said, "I'm sorry, what did you say again?"

Ethan met his gaze. "I said I'll do it. On my terms and my own way. But I'll tell the truth about who I am and get back in front of the camera as the face of *Gamers*."

Grant loosened his tie and flopped down on the leather chair across from Ethan's desk. "Jesus Christ, man. Being your friend is fucking exhausting."

Ethan smiled. "So what do you think?"

"Is this because of our argument Friday? Did I badger you?"

He held his arms out to the side. "Do I look badgered?"

Grant looked at him thoughtfully. "No, you look…happy. Actually. What the hell is going on?"

"So, I thought about what you said. And then I had a conversation over the weekend with someone special, and she said…well, she said a lot of things, but every one seemed to settle all the scattered puzzle pieces in my brain. The picture of my life is clearer, and I don't like how it is now. So I need to take steps to get to where I want to be. This is the start of that."

Grant's eyebrows lifted. "Who is this special someone?"

Ethan cleared his throat and picked up a pen, tapping it against his desk. "The photographer that was in here?"

"Lissa?"

Ethan nodded.

"Really?" Grant said. "Wow. How did that happen?"

Ethan kept it simple. "The wedding."

"Oh, right, she took photos there, too." Grant leaned his chin on his hand. "Huh. Good for you. Didn't see that one coming. But sounds like she's great for you, man. Have you told Chloe?"

Ethan shook his head. "I'll come over one night this week or over the weekend, all right?"

"Yeah, sure, she'd like that. She just wants you to be happy."

For once, Ethan could answer that with something positive. "I'm getting there."

Grant rubbed his hands together. "So, no more soul-deadening talent search? You're really going to do this?"

"Okay, don't get that evil glint in your eye, Scorsese. I told you—my terms. My way. You want me behind that camera, I call the shots. And I think it's worth it, since I'm really the most experienced and high profile candidate we've found."

Grant laughed. "You know, normally I'd tell you to shut up, but I kind of love this confidence in you. Damn right, you're the best choice. Why do you think I was such an asshole about it?"

Ethan resumed tapping his pen. "I thought at first that it might have been Chloe's voice in your ear. But you seemed so adamant about it, and you care so much about this magazine, I know you want what is best for it."

Grant nodded with a jerk of his head. "I do, and you're the best for it. You have been since you've been involved here."

"I, uh, did watch some of my old videos." Ethan cringed.

"Oh yeah?" Grant asked.

"I said some dumb shit."

Grant scoffed. "You were young. Cut yourself a break."

"Grant, I nominated a game as my Top Dawg. Spelled D-A-W-G on the screen."

His friend whistled. "Oh, that's bad."

"So bad."

"That's like, as nineties bad as the name E-Rad."

Ethan groaned. "I will not go by that name again. I'm over thirty. That's just embarrassing."

"How about E-Rogaine?"

"Shut up."

"E-AARP"

"I'm not *that* old."

"E—"

"Shut. Up. Grant."

His friend walked out of his office, whistling and pumping his fist in the air.

Ethan shook his head and tamped down the nerves that crawled over his skin like ants. He could do this. He had Grant and Chloe and Lissa at his back. With that support system, what could go wrong?

Chapter Fourteen

Ethan knocked on the door to Lissa's studio and gripped the paper bag holding their dinner tighter. He was surprising her with panini and soup from the deli down the street. She'd mentioned a couple of times how much she liked the food there. And really, it was an excuse to see her. The last time he'd seen her was when she'd stopped by his house Monday night to watch his old videos with him. And make fun of him. So now that it was Friday, he had every intention of seeing her.

A young man opened the door, and Ethan assumed he was her assistant. He wore a coat, his book bag was hitched over his shoulder, and he seemed to be on his way out. His gaze settled on Ethan's face, and then his expression brightened. "Oh, are you here for Lissa's project?"

He blinked. "The project?"

"Oh." The man's cheeks colored. "I saw the"—He waved a hand at his throat and jaw, in the same position where Ethan's scars lay on his own skin—"and thought she was taking pictures of you for her project."

Ethan didn't say a word, and the man ducked his head. "Shit, I mean. Uh, never mind."

"I'm here to see Lissa," he said, still unsure what this conversation was about, because he seemed to be missing a large piece.

"Oh, okay. She's in the studio finishing up with a client, so you can wait in her office."

Ethan nodded and murmured a "thanks." The man brushed past Ethan, and he turned to watch him as he hurried down the street, hunched against the cold. Then he turned back to the open door of the studio, his mind racing. Why would he see Ethan's scars and assume he was part of some project?

Ethan stepped over the threshold and shut the door behind him, then strode down the hallway. To the left, he glimpsed Lissa in the studio taking pictures of a young woman sitting on a stool. She glanced up at him, surprise in her eyes, and he held up the bag. "Take your time, I'll be in your office." She waved him off, taking a glance at the LCD screen on the back of her camera before resuming snapping photos.

He continued toward her office, where he closed the door behind him and sank down onto her chair. He placed the bag on a table near her desk. The unease that creeped into his veins at what Lissa's assistant said was steadily growing.

He had no intention of going through her things, but when he placed the food down, it jolted her mouse and the screensaver shut off. And what he saw on the screen froze his breath in his lungs.

It was a picture of him.

He'd been sleeping, his face in profile in his bed. She had to have taken it the morning she'd spent the night, but he couldn't understand why she hadn't told him.

He turned away quickly, his breathing turning into gasping pants as he sought to puzzle out in his head why the hell she'd taken pictures of him. And that was when his gaze landed on the white board behind her desk. There were pictures of people—all showing some sort of scars—taped to the whiteboard with a notecard next to their name. One woman had burn scars on her back and her card said, "Cindy Mathewson, 29, house fire."

If Ethan hadn't been sitting, his legs would have collapsed. His vision blurred and his head spun, because the white board was huge, taking up half of the wall and everywhere he looked. There was a note on the whiteboard: *Website launch for Rona's Scars. Monday.*

Scarred people, his picture on her computer. This mysterious project… Everything was adding up to something that made him want to throw up.

He gripped the chair, his mind fuzzy. He should leave. That's right. He should get up and walk out and then go home and…do something that made him forget about everyone, everything.

"Ethan?"

He spun the chair to see Lissa standing in the doorway. Her brows were furrowed as she took in his face, then her gaze traveled to the whiteboard behind his head, and the pictures on her computer. She sucked in a breath and her face paled, and all of that sent Ethan's stomach plummeting into his shoes.

She held out a hand. "Let me explain."

He shook his head and opened his mouth, but no sound came out, because the woman who'd pushed him to change his life, who made him happy, who got him out of this funk had been…using him? He thought she was brutally honest, but had this all been a lie? "I need to go."

"Ethan, please," Lissa pleaded. "You have to hear me out."

He jerked a thumb over his shoulder. "I think that board

explains it all. And your assistant thought I was here for your *project*." He knew his lips were curling, that his words were coming out harshly. He stood up, straightening his back to his full height, hoping it intimidated her, hoping she stepped aside so he could walk out the door. "I was always a project, wasn't I? What, help the poor scarred man come out of his shell?

But Lissa didn't back down. She never did. She spread her arms and gripped each side of the doorway so he couldn't leave. "You *will* hear me out."

He didn't want to, though. He knew himself enough to know she might as well talk to the wall, because he wasn't going to be receptive. Not while those pictures of him sleeping were right in front of his face on the computer. He didn't say a word, just glared at her.

"Originally," she said steadily, "I was going to ask you to be a part of my project, Rona's Scars. I told you about my sister. I've spent a year interviewing people with scars to share their stories, so others can read their stories and feel less alone. I'll be collecting donations for a scholarship in my sister's name. So yes, I wanted you to be a part of it. But then we got involved, and I changed my mind."

He didn't believe her anymore. So he stood like a statue as her voice began to waver. "I took those pictures of you when you were sleeping. And I'm sorry for that. Maybe it was creepy, but I wanted you to see yourself how I see you. I know those scars are more than skin deep. I know it's more than vanity, but that's not all I see when I look at you. I see—"

"A man you could use," he said bitterly. "You saw me as vulnerable."

She flinched and stepped forward, holding out her hands toward him. "Ethan, no. Please. You can't believe that. I had planned to tell you about my project before it went live. I wanted to find the right time so this, right here, didn't happen.

And I guess I waited too long—"

"You waited weeks too long," he said through gritted teeth. "And who do you think you are?" His voice was rising and he knew it. He hated it, but the fury was building and building in his gut, and he felt like he was going to burst out of his skin. "We fucked a couple of times. We spent one night together, and that gives you the right to be my therapist? Fuck you, Lissa."

He took a step forward, hoping to step past her to the door, but again she blocked it with her body. He stood there, towering over her, breathing through his nostrils so he didn't take this entire office apart with his bare hands.

Hell hath no fury like a scarred man scorned.

• • •

This had been what she'd wanted to avoid. Right now. A furious Ethan who was on the brink of a complete meltdown.

Her heart ached, because every bit of warmth that had been in his eyes when he looked at her was gone. So completely gone that she wondered if she'd imagined it in the first place.

"You have to believe me." She was faking bravado now. Deep down, she knew Ethan wouldn't hurt her, but his entire body was a coiled spring, and her instinct was to flee. She ignored that instinct.

"Was that your plan?" His voice dropped eerily low. "Sleep with me, use that tight body and sweet ass of yours to convince me to be a part of this? To allow you to take my picture and then plaster it all over the internet?"

"No," she said, her voice cracking. His words hurt her, but what hurt the most was the steel in his tone. The utter lack of…anything. "That's not true. I tried to avoid sleeping together because of this. Because I knew you'd accuse me—"

"You certainly didn't try hard."

"Maybe you were hard to resist," she shot back, getting angry now.

He scoffed. "What, do you have a scar fetish?" He pointed to a man on her board. "Did you get on your knees for him, too? Smile at him with those red lips, suck him dry, and then take his picture?"

Shit, she was shaking now, the hatred in his voice and his accusations breaking through her shield of courage. "Stop."

"What about him?" He jabbed his finger at another man. "Did you pull up your dress for him? Did you take his cock inside of you and ride him until he agreed to be some project?"

"Ethan." She gritted her teeth as the tears gathered in the corner of her eyes. "Stop. Please stop."

"Did you try to tell all of them that they were actually beautiful just so they'd agree to help you?" He took another step forward. "You're a vulture." He spat the last word and she stumbled to the side until her back hit a wall. "Delete those pictures," he said, pointing at her computer. "Delete them, because I'm not allowing you to pick at my bones. I'm done with you, and you'll be lucky if I don't find a way to shut down this project and your studio. Leave me alone."

The doorway was clear now, so Ethan took advantage of it, striding out of it without looking back. She hadn't expected him to glance her way one last time, but that didn't stop the panic from rising in her chest.

For a split second, she thought about running after him. But she'd told the truth, or what little she could think to say in the moment. If he didn't believe her, then nothing she said would do any good.

The click of his dress shoes echoed from the hallway, and then she heard the slam of the front door. She was alone now, her client having left before her conversation with Ethan, which was a blessing.

Lissa walked to her chair and sat down numbly.

She had worked so hard on all of this for Rona, and she still believed in it, still believed in the scholarship in Rona's name. But right now all she wanted to do was burn all the pictures on her white board and wipe it clean.

Her monitor caught her eye and she choked on a sob at the pictures of Ethan plastered all over it. Fumbling with the mouse through a haze of tears, she closed out all the pictures. She hadn't known Ethan was stopping by. She'd put up the whiteboard this week in anticipation for the launch, to double-check all the participants and make sure she hadn't missed anyone or confused the details. And she had been so close to choosing which pictures of Ethan to show him.

But that was ruined now. Her heart ached to think that he'd now question everything she said to him. Other than not mentioning the project, she'd been nothing less than honest. She'd been attracted to him since the moment she saw him exit his car in the *Gamers* parking lot. Before she knew who he was. Before she saw his scars. Before she knew he could light up her body with a touch of his hand and then make her laugh.

Before all of this, she'd wanted him. And she'd never meant to use him. Why couldn't he understand she'd tried to do the right thing? If only she'd told him sooner about the project, or came clean about taking pictures of him.

If only she'd done all of this differently, they'd be in her office now, talking. And later, maybe dragging out the bearskin rug for a repeat.

A paper bag sat on her desk, and she reached out slowly, unrolled the top, then peaked inside. The smell of melted cheese and hot vegetable soup wafted out from the bag. She closed her eyes as a fresh wave of tears threatened. He'd brought her sandwiches and soup from her favorite deli. He'd wanted to surprise her with dinner and his presence, and he'd left feeling used.

She took the bag and threw it in the trash, then dropped her head into her hands. She couldn't go after him now. He would still be fueled by anger. Would there be a time he'd be willing to listen to her? She wasn't so sure. And that was the worst thought of all.

Chapter Fifteen

On Monday morning, Ethan pulled on the sleeves of his suit, straightened his tie, and got in his car for the drive to work.

He'd spent all weekend testing the weak points in his armor and fixing the damage Lissa had caused. He'd told Grant they'd do a trial run on camera today, and he was prepared. He'd written out notes on notecards, and he'd shaved and even plucked a stray eyebrow hair.

He wasn't E-Rad; he wouldn't be E-Rad. Because E-Rad had feelings and loved and that wasn't Ethan. He was all business, and he was focused, and he'd never let anyone take advantage of him like Lissa had.

He gripped the steering wheel tighter as he made the turn into the parking lot of the industrial park. He knew she was launching her site today, and although he'd threatened to shut it down, he wouldn't do that. She'd said donations would go toward a scholarship, and that was the only reason he hadn't acted.

He refused to dwell on it all, though. He refused to pick apart her words, everything she'd said to him to analyze whether he thought she was telling the truth or not. He refused to do that, because he worried what he'd uncover. He worried he'd feel bad for the things he'd said to her.

So, no. He'd put it all behind him. And he'd push forward. At least he'd gotten something out of their brief time together. He'd agreed to be on camera again. But this was on his terms, his decision. He'd control the angle of the shot. Unlike Lissa's pictures. He didn't want to see himself through someone else's eyes. It was bad enough he saw himself through his own.

He strode past the conference room, where he saw a small filming area had been set up. A camera was pointed at a chair in front of a green screen. For a moment, the sight of it made him sweat, but then he steeled himself like he'd done all weekend. He could do this.

Ten minutes later, Grant sauntered into his office, rubbing his hands together. Grant had no idea that the source of Ethan's recent bout of courage had blown a hole in his confidence, so he was just as excited as he'd been last week.

"So, did you shave? Whiten your teeth? Jerk off in the shower to release tension?" Grant asked.

Ethan just glared at him.

Grant laughed. "Man, I've been thinking about this all week! I think we can do an introduction; you can talk about who you are. This doesn't have to go live for another couple of weeks, but let's rip off the Band-Aid and get you comfortable in front of the camera again, all right?"

Ethan liked that idea a whole lot, because he wasn't quite sure how he'd react when that red light was shining in his face, the lens focused on him. "Right."

Grant frowned a little, his gaze on Ethan's chest, and he looked down. "What, do I have something on my clothes?"

"Thought you'd wear some color," Grant muttered.

"This isn't even the real deal, Grant, just a trial run."

"Hey, dress for the job you want, not the job you have."

"You are so incredibly irritating."

"Yep." Grant knocked his knuckles on the desk. "So you want to do this now? Do you need a snack? Did you bring your rider?"

Ethan made a fist. "I'm going to hit you."

Grant was already strolling toward the door. "Come on, talent!"

Ethan rubbed his damp palms on his pants, surprised at his heated skin, the racing of his heart. This wasn't a big deal. It was just a camera. And it was just for practice purposes.

He straightened his suit jacket, ran a hand over his hair, and followed Grant out of his office.

In the conference room, the filming area sat in the corner. When he'd walked in that morning, his reaction had been minimal. Now, he thought it looked like a chair where they performed executions. He loosened his tie a little to get some air flowing. Was it a million degrees in here?

Back when he was E-Rad, filming was no big deal. He'd roll out of bed at noon, eat some cereal, then retreat to his cave, wearing a hoodie. Sometimes he even showered, but his hair seemed to look better if he didn't.

He'd turn on the camera, begin playing, and that was that. This was…not the same.

Grant was fiddling behind the camera, and Ethan frowned. "Don't we have someone else doing this?"

His friend didn't even look at him. "Yeah, I think Owen's gonna do it, but he's out today. I can handle a camera."

"I know you can…that's not the point."

Grant finally swiveled his head slowly. "You have a problem with me behind the camera?"

Oh, this was ridiculous. "No, certainly not."

"Okay then. Chill out and sit your ass down."

Ethan huffed and did just that, straightened the tails of his suit jacket over his thighs. Then he thought better of it and took his jacket off. He had nowhere to hang it, so he glanced around before settling it on the back of his chair. Then he checked to make sure he hadn't sweated through his shirt, which would have been gross.

By the time he glanced up, Grant was staring at him. "Dude."

"Don't call me dude."

"Are you finished primping, or…"

"Oh, just start the damn camera," Ethan snapped.

"All right," Grant said. "I'll ask you some questions just to get you loosened up, and we'll go from there."

Ethan nodded.

Grant shot him a smile and pressed a button. The red light on the front of the camera lit up, and Ethan stared at it like it was a gun pointed at his head. A bead of sweat dipped down his temple and he wiped it away as discretely as he could.

"So, why don't you tell us about yourself," Grant said.

Ethan cleared his throat, unable to look away from the glaring red light. "Hello, my name is Ethan Talley."

He didn't move, and Grant stood there for a while looking uncertain before he prompted, "Okay, and can you tell us what you used to do."

"E-Rad," Ethan blurted, as another bead of sweat trickled down his temple. Why was this whole thing sending him into a panic? He didn't know, but he couldn't stop his racing heart. "I mean, I was E-Rad." There was a five-second beat of silence before he rushed on. "I commentated video games on YouTube."

"And were you successful?" Grant asked.

Ethan blinked, but after staring into that red light, he couldn't focus well on his friend behind the camera. All he saw was a shadow and this lens and this fucking red light and holy shit, he couldn't breath. Could. Not. Breathe. Was he successful? Depended on how you defined success. "Well, I made a lot of money until I was successful at fucking up my life and killing my sister, so you tell me."

Grant slammed his hand down on top of the camera to turn it off while Ethan surged up from his chair. He was out of the conference room in three long strides, and then he was on his way to the bathroom, quickly, because he could feel his breakfast rising in his throat.

He made it to the handicapped stall and slammed the door shut in time to upchuck everything out of his stomach and into the toilet.

He stood there, leaning against the wall, toilet paper pressed to his mouth, when two black shoes appeared under the door. "E," said a deep voice.

Ethan closed his eyes and breathed deeply through his nose before tossing the paper into the toilet and flushing it. "What?"

"Can I do anything to help?"

Ethan appreciated that Grant didn't ask if he was okay. Of course he wasn't fucking okay. "I don't know."

"I can leave, or…"

"No," Ethan said, the word out before he realized what he was saying. "You…being here is good." He wasn't sure when the last time he'd wanted that. When he desired the presence of another person over being alone.

Maybe because he was tired of being alone.

He opened up the door to the bathroom stall to see Grant standing there, one hand braced on the wall. He glanced up at Ethan with round eyes. "Hey, man."

"Hey." Ethan walked to the sinks and washed his hands. "Sorry about that."

Grant leaned against the sink. "No, I feel like I'm the one who should say sorry. I pressured you into doing this, and you almost had a panic attack—"

Ethan turned to him. "You didn't pressure me into it. This

was my choice. I just hadn't…been prepared for how hard it would be, I guess."

Grant studied him for a moment. "Did Lissa give you a great pep talk?"

Ethan worked hard not to lash out. "No, we…are no longer together."

Grant made a choked sound. "What?"

He didn't understand. "It's a long story, but she was using me. Some sort of project featuring people with scars. I was a face to her. A face I thought she didn't see, when in reality, that's all she did see. I thought I would be wanted despite my scars, and she wanted me because of them. So she could take my picture and have it further her career."

Grant frowned. "Really? Chad said they're friends. I find it hard to believe she's malicious."

That was what Ethan had been trying to avoid. "Well, it's over."

"E—"

"The project launches today, in fact. Just Google 'Rona's Scars.' I didn't authorize the use of my picture, but who knows if it's up there anyway." Grant looked miserable, which Ethan empathized with. "Look, can we try again another time? I thought I pulled my shit together this weekend, but apparently I didn't."

Grant nodded. "Of course."

"And don't worry Chloe with any of this," he added.

Grant pressed his lips together, then finally said. "Fine."

Ethan turned to leave but stopped when Grant called his name. He looked at his friend over his shoulder.

"Uh…" Grant scratched the back of his neck. "I'm assuming this breakup was kind of a scene then?"

"That's safe to assume."

Grant sighed. "Yeah, okay. Maybe, uh, give this some thought once your emotions aren't so high, you know? No good decisions are made when you're pissed."

Ethan didn't want to discuss this. "The decision was sound." He pushed the door to the bathroom open as he heard Grant mutter behind him. "Of course it was."

It was. It had to be. Because the only alternative was that Ethan had fucked up another relationship in his life. He wasn't sure he could live with that.

. . .

This was supposed to be a day of celebration. A day where Lissa could sit back and honor Rona and see the product of all the hard work she'd done in her sister's honor.

And instead she was a mess, and it was all that bastard's fault. At first, she'd been devastated, hurt by his words and ravaged with guilt. She should be holding court at the bar where her parents were throwing a party for her, and instead she was hiding out in the bathroom.

Over the weekend as she'd geared up the launch of Rona's Scars, anger had taken over. Ethan had said horrible things, he hadn't believed her, and then he'd taken the happiness of this day away from her. The site had launched earlier that day. No way would she give up on her project, but not having Ethan approve was a knife in the old wound.

Taking those pictures had been a mistake, but it had been for him. She believed that in her heart, that she hadn't done it in a misguided attempt to assuage her guilt over Rona. Ethan wasn't a project. She had done it because she cared about him and wanted him to see himself through her lens.

It had backfired. In a huge, irrevocable way.

And now she sat slumped against the door of the bathroom with an ache in her muscles from tensing all weekend, staring at a cock and balls someone had drawn on the wall.

She sighed and wondered how long she could stay in here

before someone came after her when the door opened.

"Lis?" said a deep voice.

"Angel?" She turned and glared at the door as if he could see her through the metal. "What are you doing in the girls' bathroom?"

"Coming to drag you out. Now are you going to walk out on your own or do I have to make you walk?"

She rolled her eyes. "I just need a minute."

"You've had a lot of fucking minutes. I hate that this bastard did this. It's supposed to be a great day, and you're hiding out in the bathroom. Mom and Dad are worried."

Shit. He'd pulled the parent guilt trip card. After Rona's death, it was pretty much an unspoken sibling rule not to stress out their parents too much. With a growl in her throat, she unlocked the door and stomped out. Angel sat on the counter, swinging his legs back and forth as she washed her hands.

She smoothed down her dress and checked to make sure she didn't have toilet paper stuck to the bottom of her boots.

"Look, I'm not trying to be a dick—"

"I know you're not," she said. "I know that. You're kicking me in the ass, which is what you should be doing. I'm moping and it's dumb."

"He didn't taint this project. I know that's what you think, but please forget about what he said. He didn't know everything."

"Which was my fault—"

"Hey," Angel said. "Hindsight's twenty-twenty. But you know how much this project means to the subjects, and how much it will mean to recipients of this scholarship. So get your ass out there and hold your head up high."

He was right, of course, he was always right. So she did just that—straightened her spine and lifted her chin up and sauntered out of the bathroom. At the bar, her parents were standing close together, looking concerned, and Lissa hated that she'd put those looks on their faces. She smiled brightly. "Hey Mom and Dad!" She wrapped them both in a hug, her father placing his warm palm on her lower back.

"Lis," he said. "So proud of you."

Her mother held her face in her hands. "Very, very proud. The site looks great."

Lissa smiled. "Thanks. I think a reporter is supposed to be here tonight."

Her mother gestured at her outfit. "You look amazing. You'll knock 'em dead tonight."

Lissa squeezed her mom's hand. "Thanks."

An hour later, a TV reporter did in fact show up, camera in tow. They found Lissa in a corner of the bar and turned that spotlight on her. Most of the questions they fired her way were easy—talk about Rona, how she got the idea for the project, the lovely people she met along the way.

"And," the reporter said toward the end of the interview, "is there anything you want people to understand about this project?"

Lissa didn't bite her lip, because she didn't want to mess up her lipstick, so she settled for chewing the inside of her cheek as she thought of a way to formulate an answer. Ethan's face flashed through her head. "I wanted to do this for my sister and for every person who feels like she did, who struggles like she did. Every one of these people meant so much to me. I heard their stories and I felt for them, but it's not the same as actually *being* them. There are some people I met during the course of this project that aren't featured in it, and some of them were the most powerful of all." She sucked in a breath and knew she had to cut this short before she cried. "And I want to tell everyone who views this project that if I didn't get it right, I'm sorry. But I tried. I tried so, so hard."

The reporter thanked her, spoke into the camera, and

then finally that blessed red light shut off.

The camera. A pain pierced her as she remembered Ethan's vow to go back in front of the camera—stare at that red light, a changed man from the last time he'd done it.

The thought of him panicking, of hating it, made her want to throw up. She had to believe he'd been okay. That he'd made it through.

The alternative would break her heart.

For now, she turned to her family and plastered on a smile. This was her night, and she wouldn't spend time thinking about a man who hated her guts.

Chapter Sixteen

Ethan hadn't planned on looking at the site. And he'd successfully avoided it for a week, until today. Because today, he sat in his office, holding an envelope—addressed to him, care of *Gamers*—stuffed with pictures of himself.

Pictures Lissa had taken.

At first he'd been pissed but then a small note had fallen out, and in her hurried scrawl, it'd said, "How I see you. How I wish you'd see yourself."

Even after all those horrible things he'd said to her, she still had kind words. She'd taken the time to print out these photos for him. He hadn't wanted to look at them—that time on her computer was enough—but as he pulled out the five photos, his chest tightened. Because no, he certainly didn't see himself like this. He was still scarred. He was still Ethan Talley, formerly E-Rad.

But through Lissa's lens, even while sleeping, he was... peaceful. Serene. It was narcissistic, but he hadn't looked at himself for long in a mirror for years, so now he took the time to study his jawline, the curve of his ears, the profile of his nose. His bones and his complexion, the darkness of his hair, the scruff on his chin.

The scars were still there, as livid as any other day, but yet…they weren't the focal point of the photo in any way. He was the focal point. His soul.

God, this was corny, but he couldn't deny that Lissa was talented. And she'd used that talent on *him*.

He didn't know the exact address for her site, so he searched for Rona's Scars and found it right away.

He hadn't thought she'd use his photograph without permission, not really. Although he still braced himself for several days after the site went live, that someone would recognize him from it.

But no, she hadn't used his pictures, and as he scrolled through the site, he was struck by how beautiful her photos were, how heartfelt the project was, down to the color scheme, the loving way she let the subjects' own words tell their stories. The photos were similar to the ones she'd taken of him, in that the scars were always visible, but it was the soul she captured that was the focal point. How she made something invisible be visible in the picture, he had no idea, but she had.

He read the stories, and was moved by what some of these people had gone through—fires, car accidents, physical assaults, etc. They all told their stories in a way that sanded away some of his sharp edges. By the time he'd read through the site, he was sore and a little raw where the new, smoother flesh was exposed.

He leaned back in his chair and ran a hand over his face, letting it linger on the scars along his neck and jaw.

She'd said she hadn't planned on asking him to be a part of it, that their relationship had changed her mind, but yet she'd still wanted to do something for him, and the photographs sitting on his desk were what she'd done.

And he hadn't been grateful. He'd been the exact opposite

of grateful.

Sure she'd sent him the pictures, but would she be open to hearing him apologize? Because as the anger had faded the past couple of weeks, the ache of missing her had set in. There'd been so many ways they'd been good together. But how could she forgive him unless he actually made some changes?

He'd been thinking for a while, since Lissa's words at the diner, about reaching out to his parents again. He tapped his fingers on his thigh and stared at his phone. Before he second-guessed himself, he snatched it up and dialed his parents' number, one he hadn't called in a very long time but still knew by heart.

"Hello?" said his mom's voice after a couple of rings.

Ethan had to take a deep breath before he was able to talk. "Hello, it's me."

There was a pause, then her soft voice, nearly a whisper. "Ethan?"

"Yes."

"Are you okay?"

There was a sense of urgency to her tone, as if she assumed he'd only call if something was terribly wrong. There was a lot wrong, but this call was part of fixing it. "Everything's okay. I was wondering if we could get together for dinner, you and me and Dad. Maybe Chloe and Grant, too."

There was a small sound, suspiciously like a sniff. "We'd like that. It's been...so long."

Ethan ducked his head, the shame washing over him. "Yes."

"Let me talk to your father, and we'll let you know when we can have you all over. How does that sound?"

It had only taken a call. It'd been all these years, and he hadn't picked up the phone. All it had taken was a simple phone call. He had to hang up before he broke down. "Yes, that'd be fine."

"Okay then, you take care, and we'll be in touch."

"Right, talk soon." He hung up and had to take several deep breaths to get himself under control.

There were still many more words to be said, things to be aired out, but he'd made the first call, he'd initiated, and that was the first big hump.

His next task was to get back in front of that damn camera. He'd avoided it for two weeks now, but it was time to tell Grant he was ready to try again. And hopefully this time he didn't rush to the bathroom to vomit.

He stood, straightened his suit jacket, and walked to Grant's office, where the man was huddled over his cell phone. "What are you working on?" Ethan asked.

"Sexting your sister," Grant said without looking up.

Ethan wrinkled his nose. "Are you kidding me?"

Grant grinned and tossed his phone onto the desk. "I am, actually. Calm down."

Ethan rolled his eyes. "So, you ready to get the camera rolling again?"

Grant hesitated, studying Ethan's face. "Sure," he said slowly. "You want me there, or Owen?"

"Owen can handle it. If you want to observe, I won't object."

Grant stood, still keeping a careful watch on Ethan, like he thought any minute now, Ethan would spew. "You sure?"

"Yes, I'm sure."

On the way to the conference room, Grant motioned to Owen, who then stood and followed them. Owen walked toward them with raised eyebrows. He was the lead copy editor and also the boyfriend of Marley's wild-child brother, Chad. Ethan didn't understand how that worked, because the two were night and day in his opinion. But Grant said Owen had never been this focused and confident, so at least their relationship was working for him.

In the conference room, the filming area was still set up, and Ethan sauntered toward the chair, with confidence he *did* feel. He sank down as Owen stood behind the camera. He glanced at Grant, then at Ethan. "You ready?"

Ethan nodded. "I know what I'm going to say. You just make sure the camera is on."

Owen smiled slowly. "All right then. You're on in three… two…one."

Ethan began to talk.

• • •

There was a knock at her bedroom door. Lissa looked up from painting her nails. "What?"

"What're you doing?"

"Manicure."

There was a pause. "You nekkid?"

She glared at the closed door. "Of course not. Who paints their nails naked?"

Her door opened and Angel walked in, holding his laptop. "I don't know, I just didn't want to see you naked."

Lissa shook her head and returned her focus to her nails. She was perched on the end of the bed, heels on the mattress, peering over her knees as she brushed the blue polish onto her nails.

"Bright," Angel muttered.

"I like it." She glanced up to see him open up his laptop. "Uh, you needed to do whatever you're doing in my room?"

"Yeah," he said, eyes on the screen. "Because I think you're going to want to see this."

She applied polish to her last nail and then glanced up. "Fine, but I'm not getting up. I don't want to mess up my nails."

He rolled his eyes and sank down onto the bed beside

her, jostling it so she fell against him. "Hey," she said as she righted herself. "This better not be something stupid like that last video you sent me."

"That bird knew *The Addams Family* theme song. That was cool as shit!"

"Angel—"

"Okay, okay, fine, but this is nothing like that." He pulled up YouTube with a definitive tap of a key. "Here."

He held up the screen, and the first thing she saw was a thumbnail of Ethan's face. "Oh no no no." She pushed it away, but Angel held firm. "No, I'm glad he got back in front of the camera, but I don't need to see this."

Angel pushed it back toward her. "Listen, goddamnit." He tapped the track-pad and Ethan's voice filled the room. She thought for a second of putting her hands over her ears, but that was pretty immature, so instead she stared at the wall in front of her, *not* at the laptop, and listened to his deep rumble.

"It's been a long time since I've been in front of the camera. Not since I had my own channel as E-Rad. For those of you who don't recognize the name, I played video games and talked about it on camera. I did well and had over a million subscribers."

His voice was steady and calm, and she smiled a little. This had to have been hard for him. She slowly turned her head to see his image. He looked as good as he always did, dark hair slicked back, icy eyes focused.

She didn't turn away as he continued to talk. "I know I look a little different. I was in a car accident and made it out alive with some injuries, but my sister wasn't so lucky."

He took a long pause then, and she took it with him, holding her breath until he spoke again.

"So that's been a main reason for my absence. I had some grieving to do, and being on camera was the last thing on my mind. But I couldn't stay away forever from an industry I loved so much."

He went on to talk about his role at *Gamers*, and about how he planned to be a visible personality on camera.

At the end, he tilted up his chin, paused, then said firmly, "I'm sorry it's taken me so long to show my face again. It took a while for me to see anything other than the way I'd changed, and the negative ways I had done so. It took a lot of people and a talented friend to show me I was looking at it all wrong. Speaking of, if you're interested in donating to a good cause, which is personal to me and my family, please visit Rona's Scars dot org."

She inhaled sharply and her ears rang. Ethan's lips were still moving, but everything was a little fuzzy. This video had already been viewed over five hundred thousand times. And he'd just supported her project.

The video ended, and she glanced up at her brother, who was staring at her, eyebrows raised as he set his laptop to the side. "See? That's much better than a bird video."

She smacked his chest. "Angel!"

"What?"

"Angel!"

"What?!"

"I can't believe he did that."

"Well, he did do that."

She stared at the laptop.

"Lissa, that video was just released a day ago. It's all the talk in the gamer circles. E-Rad's back. And he's some big wig at a magazine now. All the gamer nerds are excited."

She held her hand over her mouth and said through her fingers, "I haven't even checked the donations recently."

"I'd suspect you have at least a little more cash in the coffers now."

She ran to her laptop to check for an updated donation

list. And sure enough, since yesterday, they'd received almost one hundred thousand dollars. "Holy shit," she whispered.

"Good?" Angel asked.

"Good?" she squeaked. "It's…it's…holy hell, gamer geeks are amazing."

Angel laughed. "He's a former leader, man. He's spoken, and he wanted everyone to support your project."

She turned to him, clutching her chest. "I think I'm going to pass out."

Her brother rushed over, took her hand, and guided her gently back to bed. "Okay, that was a lot of excitement. Why don't we take it easy?"

She lay on her pillow but then popped back up, nearly colliding with Angel. "I have to do something. I have to reach out." She'd already sent the pictures, and clearly he'd gotten them. She couldn't think of any other reason he'd been willing to lend his name to her project.

They might never be as close as they were — she suspected they never would — but they'd both made such a large impact in each others' lives. She couldn't let this silence go on any longer.

Even if she did miss him. The way he smiled at her, the trust he'd placed in her with his emotions. With his heart.

They'd made each other smile. And laugh. It didn't seem right not to reach out to him again.

"Lissa." Her brother drew out her name, like he could hear the gears turning in her head and didn't like it. "What are you concocting? He should be the one reaching out to you and groveling."

She laughed at that. "True, although I think Ethan might not be wise on ways to grovel. That little speech in his video cut his groveling time in half, gotta say."

"Damn," Angel said. "I gotta get myself famous, so I can shave off future grovel time."

"Hey." She held up a hand. "He still needs to grovel. He needs to be reminded of how good we were together." She snapped her fingers and curled her lips into what her brother called her Grinch grin. "And I think I know just the perfect thing."

Angel made a face. "Oh no, this sounds bad for him."

She stood and grabbed her purse. "Wanna come with? I need to go to the craft store."

Chapter Seventeen

It'd been a week since Ethan's first video had gone live. The response had been overwhelming. He'd expected no one to remember him, but adult gamer guys were coming out of the woodwork to reconnect with the guy they used to watch.

He did receive some condolences, and a smattering of hate here and there that he filtered out pretty well. No one could say anything worse than he'd said to himself in the past.

He kept the photos Lissa had taken of him in his desk. He looked at them, not because he wanted to see himself, but because it was the last thread of connection he had to her.

She'd posted on her site's blog recently, that she'd been surprised at the response and was so grateful that they'd have a large fund for the scholarships. He figured he was a small part of that. He hadn't heard from her, but that was okay. He hadn't boosted the signal for her project just to get her to come back to him. He'd done it because he had felt as if that was the right thing, and also because he believed in what she was doing.

Maybe one day he could tell that to her face. He'd

considered stopping by her studio so many times, but he suspected that, despite what he'd said on camera, he wouldn't be welcome.

Their secretary, Sue, knocked on his open office door. He gestured for her to come in, and she dropped the mail on his desk then left with a small wave.

He flipped through it, settling on an envelope that was addressed to him, with no return address.

The handwriting looked familiar, but he couldn't place it. With a frown, he slid his finger under the seal and opened the envelope.

There was a small sound, like the release of air, and for a moment, he saw nothing but...sparkles — a rainbow of colors as the light of his window reflected off of whatever was now surrounding him in a silent rainfall.

He blinked, blinked again, and gazed around at the complete and utter explosion that now covered his office in a tsunami of glitter.

Glitter.

Fucking everywhere.

He still held the envelope in his hands, and as he bent his head, glitter slid off his hair and onto the desk in front of him. With every small muscle twitch, more glitter fell from his body. He peered into the envelope, where a small note was tucked inside, along with some sort of plastic mechanism that had released the glitter into the air like a rocket.

He pulled out the note. All it said was: *<3 Lissa.*

He laughed. There was no other reaction, nothing to do but curl his body forward, sending more glitter fluttering to the floor, and laugh until tears fell down his glitter-covered face.

Lissa. He would have expected nothing less from her. Because this reminded him of their make-up session in her studio, of the glitter he'd found on his body days later.

As he wiped his face and stared at the craft carnage around him, he knew Lissa was just like glitter—in all his nooks and crannies and he'd never be rid of her. And he didn't really want to be rid of her.

"Holy shit." Ethan looked up to see Grant standing in the doorway of his office, eyes wide. His gaze swept over Ethan's floor and desk before resting on Ethan's face. "What the hell?"

Another laugh bubbled out of Ethan. "Lissa."

Grant blinked. "Lissa?"

He held up the envelope. "She sent me"—he spread his arms out—"this."

Grant's lips quirked up. "She glitter-bombed you?" Ethan nodded and Grant began to laugh as he nudged aside a clump of glitter with his shoe. "Wow, dude, that's…that's love."

Ethan brushed off his shoulders. "I'm not too sure about that. Could be hate."

Grant shoved his hands into his pockets and moved his foot to walk forward but then thought better of it. "Good point. So she either loves you or she hates you. You sure don't glitter-bomb anyone you feel ambivalent about." Then he took out his phone and snapped a shot. "I should send this to Chloe."

Ethan stood, sending the glitter that had been on his lap to the fall. "Well, it's not going to be a mystery much longer, because I'm definitely going to speak to her now. Even if it's to listen to her cuss me out. I can't let something as serious as a glitter-bomb go unanswered."

Grant nodded gravely. "Good luck out there, man. All's fair in love and glitter-bombing."

Ethan shook out his hair and glitter-dandruff dusted the floor. "Jesus, this is crazy. I can't leave all this for the cleaning crew."

Grant waved him off. "I'm sure I can rustle up a vacuum. I'll take care of this for you."

Ethan lifted an eyebrow. "You mean you're going to ask Marley to do it."

Grant pushed out his lips. "Uh, probably."

Ethan waved him on. "Whatever, I have to go see the person responsible for this."

As he made to walk past Grant, his friend placed a hand on his shoulder. "Hey."

Ethan stopped. "Hey what?"

Grant smiled softly. "Don't fuck it up this time."

Ethan shoved off his hand with a grin. "I'm going to do my best."

"Good luck."

"I need it."

First, he needed to shower. But then…

Then it was his turn.

· · ·

The knock on the door of Lissa's apartment startled her as she licked the brownie batter from her spoon.

She rolled her eyes, figuring it was her brother who forgot his car keys or something that he needed for work, as he'd just left for his shift.

"Coming!" she called as she padded toward the front door. She unlocked it and then opened it without even looking at who was there. "What'd you forget?" she asked as she headed back to the kitchen.

Silence greeted her question, and she slowed her steps, thinking belatedly that she hadn't confirmed the person knocking was, in fact, her brother. As she began to turn, a deep voice said, "I believe I forgot to apologize."

His words sent a flame of heat roaring through her body. She spun around to see Ethan standing in her open doorway, hands in the pockets of his jeans, the sleeves of his Henley rolled up to his elbows.

They stared at each other for a moment, and she searched her brain for something to say—it didn't even have to be witty, just something coherent to say to the man she hadn't thought she'd see again.

But damn, it was a weekend, one of the few she had off, and she couldn't think straight.

Ethan lifted his eyebrows. "May I come in?"

She swallowed. "Door's open."

His lips twitched, and then he stepped inside and shut the door behind him. He glanced around her apartment then let his gaze travel down her body. She was barefoot, wearing a pair of black leggings and an off-shoulder crop top. She had no makeup on, but at least her hair looked good.

"Hi, Lissa," Ethan said, not taking his eyes off her.

He'd probably gotten her little present in the mail yesterday or the day before. Frankly, she'd expected him to call. She had not expected him to show up at her door. "Hi, Ethan." A thought struck her. "How'd you know where I live?"

He strolled forward, picking up a picture frame on a nearby table and glancing at it before putting it back. "It's pretty easy to find someone's address nowadays."

Oh. "That's a little creepy."

He stopped and cocked his head. "It's creepy I'm here?"

She shrugged. "Not really. Not any more creepy than covering your office with glitter."

He laughed at that and continued forward until he stood a couple of feet away. He reached out a hand, and she flinched as his thumb brushed her cheek. He held up his hand, and she laughed. "Oh, uh, that's brownie batter. I like to lick the spoon."

He stuck his thumb in his mouth and took his sweet time licking off the batter. Her knees went a little weak until she remembered the last time they'd been in the same room together.

She straightened her spine and took a step back. "So why are you here?"

He must have sensed the change in her, because he dropped the act, and tension crept into his expression. "I have some things I want to say to you."

She turned and walked into her kitchen, Ethan following her, and proceeded to fill the pan with brownie batter. He didn't talk for a moment, and she glanced over her shoulder to see him standing awkwardly by the refrigerator. "So? Talk."

A muscle in his jaw ticked, and the sign of his irritation pleased her. He blew out a breath and ran his fingers through his hair. "I know I don't deserve it, after the things I said, but would you please turn around and look at me."

She placed the pan of brownies in the oven, set the timer, and then turned around, leaning back on the counter. She brushed her hair out of her face and gazed at him steadily.

He inclined his head. "Thank you."

"You're welcome."

He hesitated a moment then said, "I'm sorry."

Those two words hung in the air between them, and Lissa waited to see if they came with a caveat, a but, anything really. But there were no strings attached to those words, and she knew that based on the way Ethan was looking at her with a resolved expression. Those words were hers now.

She stared at a point over Ethan's shoulder. "I was in the office at *Gamers*, staring out a window, when a black SUV pulled into the parking lot. A man got out of the car and I... couldn't look away from him. It was the way he held himself, the way he walked, the way he looked. Everything about him intrigued me. I was attracted to him before I knew who he was." She met Ethan's ice-blue eyes. "And then I found out who he was, that he was the man I'd been hoping to meet, to ask him to be a part of my project. I told myself not to get involved with him, because I didn't want to be accused of whoring myself out." Ethan winced and opened his mouth, but she kept talking. "But I was still attracted to him, and when he pursued me, I couldn't turn him down. I kept thinking it was okay. It was just casual. Until it stopped being just casual. Because it did stop, right? It became more."

Ethan swallowed. And nodded.

She gripped the edge of the countertop as her stomach rolled. "So I knew then I couldn't do it. I couldn't ask him, not after everything he'd confided in me. But I still wanted to do something for him. I-I'm sorry, too."

Ethan jolted forward. "No, Lis—"

She shook her head. "I don't regret taking those pictures of you. I regret you finding out the way you did." She paused to see if he'd protest, but he stayed silent so she could continue. "I wanted to do something for you. A surprise. For you to see you how I see you. I wanted to help. And it backfired. And I'm sorry for the part I played in that."

Ethan's fingers twitched where they rested against his thighs. "Can I—can I come to you?"

The hesitation and vulnerability in his voice pierced her. "Of course," she whispered.

In two long strides, he was in her space, his one hand resting on her hip while the other cupped her neck. "I owe you the apology. The things I said…I can't think about them without cringing, without regretting it all. I looked at your project and it affected me. I felt what those people felt, and I read their stories and internalized it all. It was good work, amazing work, and I know it's making an impact in people's lives."

She hadn't realized how much she wanted to hear that from him until he'd said it. "Ethan—"

"I'm sorry. I'm so sorry, because I fucked up the only

thing that's made me happy in years. And worse than that, I hurt you. And that's something I would do anything to atone for."

She pressed her lips together. "This apology is doing wonders."

A flicker of hope came into his eyes. "Yeah?"

She nodded. "And maybe some pics of your office. Covered in glitter."

He smiled. "Grant has one on his phone."

"He'll have to send it to me." She ducked her head and pulled out of his grip, because while the apology was great, it was hard to feel his touch knowing it wouldn't lead further. She busied herself cleaning up, her back to him. "Thanks for coming by. You could have called."

He didn't answer, and she scrubbed at a spot on the counter that she knew was a permanent stain, but it was the only thing she could focus on, knowing he was still there in her apartment.

"Lissa," he said softly.

She wiped harder.

A hand settled on her elbow, stilling her. "Lissa. Please turn around."

She tossed the wipe with a huff and turned slowly, refusing to look up, and stared straight ahead at the base of his neck.

That is, until he placed a hand on her chin and forced her meet his gaze.

After a moment, he spoke. "I didn't come here just to apologize. I came here to ask you if you'd give me another shot. Give *us* another shot."

So that was what she'd wanted to hear. Because with his eyes on her, those words settling down into her bones and heating her blood, she knew for certain that, despite everything, she wanted exactly that.

As she'd been falling for the way he touched her body,

she'd also been falling for him—for the rare moments of vulnerability he showed, the way he laughed when they were together, the way conversation with him was easy.

He soothed over the pain she'd felt for so long after the death of her sister, and she thought maybe she did the same thing for him, too.

His eyes were still searching hers, clearly waiting for an answer. She bit her lip. "Should I leave you hanging?"

He chuckled softly. "I wish you wouldn't."

She gripped his face, the stubble of his beard rubbing her palms. "Will you promise to make that sound a lot?"

"What sound?"

"Laughter." His face grew tender at her words. "I like to hear you laugh."

He leaned in to her touch. "I missed laughing. Around you, it's easy to do it again."

She nudged his nose with hers. "And I missed your grumpy face."

Ethan hesitated then leaned in and pressed a soft kiss to her lips. "I missed that, too."

She pursed her lips. "Oh yeah? What else?"

With a quick motion, he scooped her up and placed her on the counter, then stepped between her legs. He slid her shirt further down her arm, along with the strap of her tank top. He watched her face, as if he was waiting to see if she'd stop him, but no way. *No way*. Not when she felt the hard ridge of his arousal between her legs, not while her body was heating up just from his simple touch.

He pressed a kiss to her shoulder then ran his tongue along her collarbone to the rounded top of her breast. "I missed this skin right here."

She gripped his hair and shifted closer, making it clear she wanted more. He smiled up at her then lifted her shirt and tank top over her head, leaving her topless. Her nipples peaked in the cool air, but Ethan didn't leave her hanging for long. He dipped his head and took a stiff bud into his mouth, sucking and rolling it between his teeth.

She groaned. "Oh shit, I missed this, too. So much."

He pulled back and cupped her breasts. "We never had a problem when we were doing this."

She shook her head and bit her lip as he leaned in to press a line of kisses down her neck. "Okay, you need to take me to my room now, because I'm feeling the urge to get a lot more naked."

He chuckled against her skin then lifted her off the counter. She wrapped her legs around his waist and directed him to her bedroom. They only bumped into a couple of walls on the way.

As he walked through her doorway, she sucked his earlobe and his breath hitched. He tossed her onto the bed and pointed at her sternly. "Get naked."

She lifted herself up onto her elbows and watched as he proceeded to drop his clothes in seconds. With a stretch, she took a condom from her bedside drawer.

It'd been a while, and they were both hot and aching for it, so Ethan didn't waste time as he rolled the condom down his length and then settled himself between her legs. His jaw was tight as he gazed down at her, bracing himself on his forearms. "I'm sorry, I'm—"

She gripped his ass and tugged. "No need to talk or apologize, just fuck me already."

He laughed and mumbled against her lips. "Fuck, I really, really missed you." And then he thrust into her.

The force of it slammed her eyes shut, and she moaned as he filled her. He panted above her as he began to fuck, and she got a tight grip on his ass, digging her nails into his flesh. His grunt told her he liked it.

She opened her eyes to see him gazing down her body at

their connection. He lifted his head, a lock of hair falling into his eyes, and smiled.

She smiled back, thrusting her hips to meet his. A gasp left his lips, and for moments, they moved in sync, like they were made to do this together. Tension began to creep into Ethan's body and she knew he was close, just as she was. In this position, he hit all her spots, and with another couple of thrusts, she was coming, with Ethan soon following.

For long moments they lay entwined, not speaking, just breathing.

Finally, Ethan kissed her forehead and pulled away to go to the bathroom. He didn't know where the bathroom was, so he stumbled around until Lissa took pity on him.

When he came back into the bedroom, he climbed into bed, wrapping an arm around her stomach. "The timer beeped. I took out your brownies to cool."

She smiled as she ran her nails up and down his arm. "My hero." After a pause, she asked, "So how big is this shot?"

He frowned. "What do you mean?"

"Are we all in? Or—"

He rolled onto his back with a yawn and scratched his chest absentmindedly. "We're spend-nights-together, meet-the-family kind of all in."

"Meet the family?" she squeaked.

He glanced at the clock. "We got a couple of hours."

"A couple of hours?" She surged up with a hand planted on the bed. "What're you talking about?"

He seemed unaffected by her alarm. "We have dinner with my parents soon."

She worked on her breathing. "I'm sorry, what?"

Finally, an emotion flickered over his features. Unease. "I, uh, reached out to my parents. This will be the first time I'll have seen them in years." He met her gaze. "I'd like you there with me, please. By my side."

Oh God, how could she say no to that? Even though she wanted to vomit at the thought of meeting his parents already, he wanted her support. "Had you planned on asking me that before you showed up here?"

He shook his head. "No, I kinda just decided that five minutes ago. Because now that I convinced you take me back, I can't imagine going over there without you. I know it's a lot to ask but…please?"

She smiled and collapsed back on her side then rested her chin on his chest. "I'm a big girl. I can handle myself. You want me by your side, I'm there."

He ran a thumb over her lips as he gazed at her with undisguised adoration. It warmed her down to her toes. "What'd I do to deserve you?"

"Had sex with me on a glitter-covered bearskin rug."

He laughed, which made her head bob where it rested on him. "For the record, I'm still picking glitter out of places glitter shouldn't be."

She curled her lips between her teeth.

He narrowed his eyes. "You think it's funny."

She shook her head.

He grew still, and she had a second to squeal and try to squirm away before he grabbed her and began tickling her, then he began doing other things with his hands, and she stopped trying to get away from that.

Chapter Eighteen

Ethan hadn't been to his parents' house in…well, it'd been a long time. And now he stood at their front door, his clammy hand in Lissa's, hoping he didn't throw up.

As for Lissa—his woman stood with a straight back, lifted chin, gripping his hand tightly. She might have been faking it, but she looked confident as hell. Today, she wore a simple teal dress, nude heels and a large chunky necklace. She'd clipped back one side of her hair, and everything about her was beautiful and comforting. She turned her head, catching him watching her, and winked.

He smiled and tugged her closer, pressing a kiss to her lips, and that's when the front door opened.

He broke apart quickly, not because he was embarrassed to kiss his girlfriend—yes, girlfriend—in front of his mother, but because he preferred not to be sucking face when she saw him again for the first time.

There was a small intake of breath, and when Ethan straightened his shirt and looked at his mother, she stood on the doorstep, one hand on her chest, gazing back and forth between Ethan and Lissa, then down to their clasped hands.

She blinked rapidly. And Ethan swallowed. Because what was there to say to his estranged parents? So he said, "Hello, this is Lissa Kingsman. And if you want to give someone credit for me finally calling you, it should be her."

Lissa turned to him with a frown. "No, that's not true."

"Yes, it is."

She shook her head, let go of his hand so she could place hers on her hips, and faced him. "No, you need to give yourself some credit for picking up the phone. I wasn't there when you did that. I wasn't even speaking to you then, actually."

"But I don't think I would have called if I hadn't met you."

"Okay, maybe I'll take that tiny bit of credit. She held up her fingers a millimeter apart and raised the tone of her voice. "A teeny tiny bit."

He threw up his hands. "Are we really arguing about this right now on my parents' front porch?"

Lissa's eyes widened and she snapped to attention, facing his mother. "Oh shit, uh, shoot. Sorry Mrs. Talley." She brushed her hand over her hair. "Wow, what you must think of me." She smacked Ethan's stomach lightly with the back of her hand. "Face your mother and hug her or something. We can still salvage this."

Ethan rolled his eyes and was about to retort when a snuffling noise caught his attention. He turned to his mother, who was now holding a hand over her mouth and she was… laughing.

Really laughing, as in, chest shaking, tear-inducing shaking. She managed to get herself under control enough to hold out her arms, which Ethan stepped into quickly. She hugged tight, pressing a kiss to his cheek. He closed his eyes as he scented her familiar perfume on her skin. "Hi, Mom."

She pulled back and wiped away the lipstick stain she'd left behind. "Hi, Ethan." Her voice trembled a little, and she cleared it before turning to Lissa. She, too, received a Talley hug, and smiled at him over his mother's shoulder.

"Thank you for bringing him to us," she said, and Lissa only nodded, her eyes a little wet.

Inside, Ethan's father sat on his recliner, talking to Grant and Chloe. Ethan's sister whirled around as Ethan walked into the room, and Ethan wanted to cry at the pure joy on her face.

Why hadn't he given this to her earlier? To his parents? Hell, to himself?

Ethan's father watched him a little warily. It had been a long time, after all. Then he held out his hand, a brief smile crossing his face as Ethan clasped it and shook.

He sat down on the loveseat in the living room, Lissa beside him.

"Thanks for having us," Ethan said. "I know it's been a long time but"—he rolled his jaw—"I needed that time."

His mother drew her lips between her teeth as his father watched him steadily. "I think we needed the time, too, Ethan. What matters is that we made the first step to all be together again. I have hope we can…find a new normal."

Lissa's hand slipped into his, and he squeezed it. "Yes, I think we can."

During dinner, his parents enjoyed shooting rapid-fire questions at Lissa. About her life and her family and job. They especially had a lot of questions about Rona's Scars. Ethan worried it was too much, but Lissa seemed to flourish under the attention. She poured on the charm so thick, he knew she was about to take over the coveted favorite spot from Grant.

"Ethan," his father said, "Chloe showed us you're back in front of the camera now."

He nodded. "It was a hard decision, but now that I've done it, I certainly don't regret it."

"You sounded great," his mother interjected. "And

looked very handsome."

He laughed softly. "Thanks, Mom."

"The videos are getting more attention than we even expected," Grant said. "We have requests for Ethan to demo games and possibly even make a throwback video to the time he was E-Rad."

"This game is a Top Dawg!" Lissa said in a low voice.

He glared at her. "I did not sound like that."

She took a sip of her water. "Uh, yeah you did."

"You did," Chloe said, giggling.

Ethan sighed. "The women are ganging up on me. We'll see who I decide to call out on camera next video, hmmm."

"Bring it," Lissa said, nudging him with her elbow.

After dinner, Ethan made a quick trip to the bathroom, and on the way back, his father met him in the hallway. "Could I speak to you for a moment?"

Ethan had figured this was coming. He couldn't use Lissa as a buffer forever. "Yes, of course."

His father gestured for him to step into an office, which Ethan did, glancing around at the dark oak furniture and dusty books. He shuffled his feet and turned around to face his father, who was watching him intently. "So, why did you decide to call us now?"

Ethan laughed softly. "Don't beat around the bush, Dad, Christ."

His dad shrugged, with a smile.

Ethan ran his hands through his hair. "I've been punishing myself for years. And seeing you mourn also made me feel even worse."

His father stared at the floor. "We didn't know what to say to you. I know we failed, but we're only human. We were angry and…it was hard."

He shook his head. "No, I understand. I cut myself off from you, because it was the only way to cauterize the wound."

His father looked up. "And now?"

"And now…well Lissa has had a loss in her life, too. And her family rallied. They all took some blame for her sister's death, but they didn't fracture, they glued themselves together into a different picture. I want that for us."

His father stepped forward and clasped Ethan in a hug. "I want that, too, son."

Ethan squeezed his father, then they both stepped back, clearing their throats awkwardly after that display of affection. Ethan's father nodded toward the door. "So, dessert?"

Ethan grinned. "Yeah, dessert sounds good."

• • •

Lissa watched as Ethan swirled his spoon in a lake of whipped cream on his plate then scooped up a berry and slipped it into his mouth. Grant said something funny, and Ethan laughed, his face flushed from wine.

He'd never be the same man he was when he was E-Rad, just as she wasn't the same woman she was back then, either. But this Ethan was an improvement over the one she first met in the *Gamers* office. This Ethan laughed and talked more, scowled less, and was…happier.

He told her she was a huge reason for that, but she knew she was just the catalyst, really. He did everything else on his own, from getting in front of the camera again to reconciling with his parents.

He glanced at her. "You need more wine? Another slice of cake?"

She shook her head, still gazing at him with what she knew was undisguised adoration. "No, I'm good."

He reached out and rested his hand on hers where she held her wineglass. "I told you how beautiful you look today, right?"

She smiled. "Yeah, you did."

He nodded. "Just checking."

A soft sigh made Lissa look up, to see Chloe watching them with her hands clasped to her chest.

"You look like you're an extra in a Disney movie, Chloe," Grant said. "Maybe tone down the gasping and the staring, huh?"

Chloe glared at him. "I'm observing romance in real time here, Grant. Mind your own business."

He rolled his eyes then winked at Lissa when Chloe wasn't looking.

Lissa hadn't known what to expect at all before she met Ethan's family, but they had fully accepted her. She assumed it had a lot to do with her encouraging Ethan to come back into their lives, but they had also seemed interested in her life.

She'd been back with Ethan for about a day, but already it seemed as if they had been together much longer.

When they finally said their good-byes to his family, they walked hand-in-hand. Lissa tried to unclasp her hand so she could get in the car, but Ethan wouldn't let go. "The weather's nice, right? Want to take a walk?"

She glanced down at her heels. "Let me grab my flats out of the car, okay?"

He motioned to her to wait, and so she did, as he retrieved her shoes from the car. He bent over, taking off her heels and then slipping her flats onto her feet, then he placed her heels gently on the floor of the car. "You ready?"

Chloe had been right. This was romance. "You know I'm a sure thing, right?"

Ethan cocked his head. "What?"

"As in, I already agreed to put up with you. I'll be getting naked with you tonight, I'm sure, and I'll probably be the one begging for you to fuck me again in the morning. You don't have to do all this." She motioned to her feet.

He didn't move for a minute, and then he laughed, his voice echoing off the brick wall of the house. Lissa glanced back and saw a curtain in the Talley house move. Well, crap, hopefully no one heard her talking about fucking.

She turned back to Ethan, who was wiping his eyes. "Lissa, you are without a doubt the woman for me."

"What did I say that was so funny?"

He stepped toward her and gripped her hands between them. "I wanted to romance you because you deserve it. Because I didn't from the beginning."

"You don't have to make up for anyth—"

"I don't think that. There's no quota for me to fill. I want to treat you well, romance you, sweep you off your feet, because that's what feels right. You make me so happy, that all I want to do is make you happy, too."

Oh, she was going to cry. "Ethan—"

"I do make you happy, right?"

She cradled his jaw with her palm. "Of course you do. I love that I was the one to finally smooth this line on your forehead." She ran a finger over his scowl line. "And get these to turn up." She pressed on a corner of his lips and he feigned biting her. She laughed softly. "You make me feel wanted and needed and also really horny."

He surged forward to kiss her then mumbled against her lips. "Let's forget that walk and get home and get naked."

She nodded frantically as she squeezed his ass. "That's a great plan."

Epilogue

Ethan hunched over the handlebars of his cart and sighed. Lissa stood in front of a row of Crock-Pots, her hands on her hips. "So, this one would go with my parents' kitchen, because it's blue, but this one is programmable." She turned to him. "What do you think?"

He just stared at her, and she rolled her eyes. "You're a Grinch."

"I dislike crowds," he huffed.

She smiled. "You're so cute when you're grumpy."

"How about I be extra grumpy and we get out of here and get naked?"

She laughed. "There are small children around, you weirdo, stop."

He pursed his lips as Lissa turned back to studying the Crock-Pots. They were shopping for Christmas presents. Ethan would have ordered everything online at the last minute, but Lissa wasn't having that. She said she needed to "see things in person" before she purchased them.

So that was why he found himself pushing an already full

cart around Target, with Lissa in the lead.

She finally grabbed a box and tossed it into the cart, then scanned the list on her phone. "Okay, my parents down. Let's do yours now. I'm thinking a Keurig. They have room on their counter, and they never make the whole pot of coffee." She bit her lip. "What do you think?"

"I think," he began but then stopped as he took time to take in the moment. He was shopping. For his parents. For the first time in years. He was with a woman he loved with all of his heart, a woman who had convinced him to better his life.

He was bitching about shopping and how his feet hurt, and he hadn't realized just how special this was. How years ago he didn't have this. He had people he loved to shop for, and that meant something. He swallowed around the lump in his throat, and his voice was hoarse as he said, "Yeah, I think that's a great idea."

Lissa studied his face and then stepped beside him, placing her hand on his arm. "You okay?"

He nodded. "Yes, i-it just kind of hit me now, how I haven't bought my parents a Christmas present for years, and now I'm here with you. Shopping for our families. That I'm in a relationship with a woman as special as you, who notices and thinks about what kind of present my parents would appreciate." He shook his head as Lissa's eyes widened. "Fuck, I love you."

Her lips trembled. "Are you seriously making me cry right now? In Target the week before Christmas?"

She smacked his arm and he started to laugh. "I'm sorry!"

"You jerk!" she huffed, but her tone was affectionate. "Stop, stop it right now. I don't want to cry in front of the Crock-Pots."

"I love you," he said again.

"I love you, too," she said. "Now let's go pick out a Keurig."

• • •

Lissa watched as Ethan shoved the last of the presents they'd bought that afternoon into the hall closet. "Did they fit?" she called from the living room. She'd moved in about a month ago. Ethan had asked her the day after they agreed to get back together, and she'd managed to hold him off for a while. He'd finally put his foot down, because he wanted her there all the time. And to be honest, she wanted to be there.

He shut the door and made his way toward her. "We bought a lot of things."

"Yeah, well, you're a star now, making big bucks."

He rolled his eyes at her, but it was true. Ethan as the face of *Gamers* was just about the best thing that had happened to the magazine, and to Ethan. He could still be a grumpy guy sometimes, but on camera, he really came alive.

He sank down on the couch beside her. "Look who's talking?"

Not only had they already received all the funding for the first Rona Kingsman scholarship, but Lissa's studio business had picked up. "I'm not as famous as you."

He shrugged. "I only care about being famous to you."

She laughed. "Oh, you're famous to me all right, baby."

He grinned. "So, remind me again of the holiday schedule."

She held up her hand and ticked off her fingers. "Christmas Eve is with Grant, Chloe, Sydney, Austin, and Marley. Christmas morning is with my parents. Christmas afternoon and evening is with your parents. The day after Christmas is my family reunion."

"Who holds family reunions the day after Chistmas?"

"The Kingsmans," she answered. "And I already told them you're coming and the kids are excited."

"Oh God," he muttered. "Am I going to have to sit at the kiddie table?"

She swung her legs up so they rested on his lap, and then reclined on the sofa. "If you do, I'll make it up to you, I promise."

He rested his hand on her feet. "Oh, really? Hmm, actually I really want you to have to make something up to me. I'll volunteer to sit with the kids."

She laughed. "You're ridiculous."

He began to massage her feet as he kept his gaze on her face. "The holidays will be busy for us this year."

"Yes," she said on a moan as he hit a knot in her arch.

"And you know what?"

"Hm," she answered, her eyes closing.

"I'm grateful for that."

She opened her eyes. "Yeah?"

He smiled. "Yeah and I promise not to be a Grinch. Much."

She sank down further into the couch, with a smile. "Sure, whatever you say, Ethan. I'll love you anyway."

A chuckle reached her ears. "Yeah, I know."

Acknowledgments

This series has been such a joy for me. The idea for the first book came to me on a whim, and I couldn't stop writing it. I had fun challenging myself with a different story structure and adult themes. And I loved being an Entangled author!

Thanks so much to my editor, Heather Howland for working with me on this series. For caring about these characters as much as I did, and for working with me through countless edits until we got it right. Also, thanks for encouraging me to write about glitter!

Thanks to my agent, Marisa Corvisiero. Having you in my ring is so so comforting. You know me and this business and on top of that, you're fun to hang out with!

Thanks so much to Nana Malone for talking me through some aspects of this book and for introducing me to Curly Nikki! I have spent way too much time on that blog!

Thank you to my writing friends, because I could not do this without you. Thank you to my Mobsters, who have been champions for Ethan from the beginning.

And thanks to my family, who put up with my absences while I'm knee-deep in characters and conflict. I love you!

About the Author

Megan Erickson worked as a journalist covering real-life dramas before she decided she liked writing her own endings better and switched to fiction.

She lives in Pennsylvania with her husband, two kids and two cats. When she's not tapping away on her laptop, she's probably listening to the characters in her head who won't stop talking.

For more, visit www.meganerickson.org or sign up for her newsletter at eepurl.com/KNN9P

Discover the **Gamers** *series...*

CHANGING HIS GAME

Getting caught with a dirty GIF by the smoking-hot IT guy is a whole new level of awkward for Marley Lake. What she doesn't know is that Austin Rivers is a secret partner—and technically her boss. One look at that GIF, though, and he's ready to install a lot more than just software. But with Marley's promotion and reputation on the line, Austin will have to find a way to change his game...or risk losing the only woman with the cheat code to his heart.

PLAYING FOR HER HEART

Grant Osprey just had the hottest sex of his life. Sure, they were both in costume, and yes, it was anonymous, but he never expected her to bolt without exchanging names. Then he meets his business partner's little sister. Chloe Talley isn't the bold, sexy vixen he remembers. And she wants nothing to do with him—unless they're role-playing. Each scene pushes her beyond her strict boundaries, forcing her to face why she can't be with *anyone*, let alone Grant, until he demands the one character Chloe *can't* play. Herself.

TIED TO TROUBLE

When Chad Lake spots a sexy nerd at his sister's party, he can't resist trying to ruffle the guy's bow tie. But in the end, it's Chad who's left wide-eyed, his ears still ringing with the filthy things the guy whispered in his ear. Owen's heard *all* about the cocky Adonis, and he has every intention of steering clear of the man—until Chad's sexy taunts push him too far. There's something intriguing about Chad, though, and even though Owen knows the infuriating man is trouble, he can't seem to stay away...

If you love sexy romance, one-click these steamy Brazen releases...

TAKING THE SCORE
a *Tall, Dark, and Texan* novel by Kate Meader

Paying down her sister's debts left personal assistant Emma Strickland with little more than the thrift store suit on her back and a second job as a waitress in a strip club. She'll do anything to keep her uptight, sexy-as-hell boss Brody Kane from finding out. But when he brings an important client to the club and gets the worst lap dance in adult entertainment history—from her— Brody makes it his mission to uncover her secrets, one illicit, over-the-desk encounter at a time.

OVER THE TOP
a *Maverick Montana* novel by Rebecca Zanetti

Dawn Freeze had a huge crush on Hawk Rain for years. That tall, lean body. Intense dark eyes. And always one foot out the door. Now he's on leave for exactly one week. And this time, he's made it crystal clear that he only wants one thing. *Her.* But just as Hawk allows himself one mindblowingly intense night with Dawn, he learns that everyone he loves is in danger. *Especially* her. And the only way to protect Dawn is to push her away...

SEDUCING THE FIREMAN
a *Risky Business* novel by Jennifer Bonds

Firefighter Jackson Hart is back in Brooklyn and on the hunt for the girl who's kept him burning for ten long years. The girl he left, in a total prick move, without saying goodbye. He's determined to make it up to her, but Becca's not ready to forgive and forget. Good thing Jax isn't the kind of man to give up when he wants something. And he *always* gets what he wants.

LIGHT HER FIRE

a *Private Pleasures* novel by Samanthe Beck

Good girl Melody Merritt is ready to be *bad*. And who better to burn her sterling reputation to the ground than Bluelick's sinfully sexy new fire chief? Corrupting the prim and proper beauty is the most action Josh Bradley's seen since transferring from Cincinnati to fast-track his career, but he won't let *anyone* — not even the delectable Melody Merritt — trap him in this Kentucky-fried Mayberry. Too bad he's started a blaze that's completely beyond his control...